ALSO BY PIERRE KLOSSOWSKI

Sade My Neighbor
Roberte ce soir and The Revocation of the Edict of Nantes
Diana in Her Bath and The Women of Rome
Such a Deathly Desire
The Baphomet
Nietzsche and the Vicious Circle
Living Currency

THE SUSPENDED VOCATION

THE SUSPENDED VOCATION

PIERRE KLOSSOWSKI

TRANSLATED BY JEREMY M. DAVIES
AND ANNA FITZGERALD

WITH AN INTRODUCTION BY BRIAN EVENSON

Copyright © 1950 by Éditions Gallimard
Translation copyright © 2020 by Jeremy M. Davies and Anna Fitzgerald
All rights reserved
First edition, 2020

Library of Congress Cataloging-in-Publication Data
ISBN: 978-1-7348382-0-6
Designed by Eric Wrenn Office
Typeset in Sabon

Printed in Turkey
http://www.smallpressnyc.com

For Brice Parain

"We struggle not against flesh and blood, but against the spiritual power of wickedness in high places."

—Eph. 6:12

INTRODUCTION

There are certain literary figures who establish themselves in the public eye, who become over time readily identifiable as the face of a movement. It's almost impossible now to talk about existentialism without thinking of Jean-Paul Sartre, for instance, or to think of literary modernism without James Joyce and Virginia Woolf springing quickly to mind. Once you begin to interest yourself in a movement or school and dig deeper, however—once you begin to consider how a literary or philosophical movement developed—other figures start to gain prominence. You begin to realize that there are other people who were crucial to the development of, say, modernism—indeed, were once seen as central—but faded from visibility with time: Wyndham Lewis or Henry Green or Dorothy Richardson, for instance.

And then there are those figures who seem to flit around the edges of movements without ever being fully involved in any of them, who pursue their own eccentric paths no matter what is going on around them. These are the writers who make up the secret history of literature, the hidden history that's not easily reduced to movements or trends, and who always waver on the verge of invisibility until you stumble by accident onto one of their books and realize how good they actually are, and wonder Why wasn't I told to read this before? But of course you already know the answer: you were not told because it doesn't fit smoothly into the story those in authority made up about what literature is—it disrupts, it can't be reduced to the literary equivalent of a meme.

That's the kind of writer Pierre Klossowski (1905–2001) is. He is not a joiner. He has his own particular and often peculiar concerns, and pursues them. He does not particularly welcome you in. The content of his writing, too, has the feel of a gnostic text, as if you are reading something that, if only you were properly initiated, you would understand in a different way. In that sense his work has an esoteric or occult quality to it—and likewise in the sense that it returns again and again to the intersection of religion and pornography, the sacred and the profane.

This is not to say that Klossowski was standoffish. One of the interesting things about him is that once you finally notice him you begin to see his shadowy presence everywhere in twentieth-century French culture. He was, for instance, an early French translator of Walter Benjamin—as well as Wittgenstein, Heidegger, and Kafka, among others. When very young, he was a secretary for André Gide and appears semidisguised as a character in Gide's novel *The Counterfeiters*, a novel he appears to have helped edit and for which he also made illustrations (which were turned down for being too overtly erotic). The older brother of the painter Balthasar Klossowski de Rola, better known as Balthus, Klossowski was an artist himself, and his work is at once naïve and pornographically explicit in a way that sometimes references occult texts, mythology, and Klossowski's own prose. He was a friend of Georges Bataille—and indeed Bataille's own investigation of erotism might best be read in counterpoint to Klossowski. He was involved marginally with surrealists, spent time in a Dominican seminary, was later involved with the existentialists, and wrote philosophical texts on Friedrich Nietzsche and the Marquis de Sade that were influential for post-structuralism. His book-length economico-philosophical essay *La Monnaie vivant* (*Living Currency*) Foucault called "the best book of our times." Fiction writer, philosopher, translator, and visual artist, Klossowski worked in many modes and media and seemed to touch the lives of many of the literary and artistic figures we now admire. Indeed, once he's noticed, it's hard not to suspect he's lurking even where you don't see him.

American readers are not likely to know Klossowski's work, though a number of his books have been published in English translation, mostly by small or academic presses. They may be slightly more likely to know Klossowski's art, but usually as a kind of annex to the artwork of his more famous (and equally controversial) brother Balthus. His first novel *La vocation suspendue*, here admirably and lucidly translated by Anna Fitzgerald and Jeremy M. Davies as *The Suspended Vocation*, is perhaps best known in the Anglophone world, if at all, through the remarkably faithful if loose adaptation scripted and filmed by the Chilean-French director Raúl Ruiz in 1978. The metafictional conceit of *The Suspended Vocation* (of which more below) would seem to make a movie version quite impossible, but Ruiz rises to the occasion by utilizing different actors and film stocks to represent the same characters and situations in differing interpretations.

Klossowski's novel is the story of internecine conflict within the Catholic Church hierarchy. At the center of the story is Jérôme, a seminarian who finds himself in the center of a power struggle in which he's not really sure of the sides or the players, in which any given individual might be sincere or might be hiding their true nature (if there is such a thing as true nature), and in which his own assumptions about where others stand, how they communicate with one another, and what he himself should do, end up putting him increasingly at odds not only with those around him but with himself. There seems to be a sect called "The Devotion," as well as a sinister, authoritarian order called "The Black Party"—though we are sometimes told that this latter does not, in fact, exist, or might indeed be the official "Inquisitorial arm of the Church." Klossowski's narrator extrapolates that "[one] religious order (never explicitly named) able to exercise spiritual terror within the Church [is vying] with a rival order over the question of methods . . ." The latter group is "like a serpent with coils everywhere, whose segments always reunite," which seems to have become perhaps unhealthily invested in a folk ritual known as "Our Lady of the White Marriage," the obscure details of which will eventually seem to be hinted at in a religious fresco that causes Jérôme no end of trouble. Add to that Jérôme's past life and indiscretions; his former friend and rival Malagrida, a painter; his taciturn spiritual advisor; the louche puppet-master La Montagne (which translates as "The Mountain"); a nun named Mother Angélique, who may or may not be on his side; the seeming heresies of an atheistic priest; and countless other men of the cloth whom Jérôme has difficulty understanding and who may be saying things they don't actually believe in order to see what he might say back to them . . .

Confused yet? It's a little like a John le Carré novel in which anyone might be a double or even triple agent, but instead of spies you have priests and nuns and much of the plot and overt explanation has been drained away. *The Suspended Vocation* is a difficult text in that it keeps the reader in the same suspended uncertainty that Jérôme is in, and asks us to experience his struggle and confusion. In that sense, it strikes me as less of a descriptive text than an experiential one. It is as if, in reading it, you are ritually undergoing Jérôme's struggle and moving toward the revelation that will most unsettle him.

And yet, you go through it at one remove: Klossowski's *The Suspended Vocation* presents itself as a long critical review of a book (that does not exist) also called *The Suspended Vocation*. The author of the review has strong opinions about that book, makes guesses about what the author intended, and harbors suspicions as to the relationship of what's going on in the text to the politics of the 1940s. In other words, *The Suspended Vocation* is an interpretation/analysis of this other *The Suspended Vocation*, which is about Jérôme's struggles (and, I would argue, ultimately his failure) to interpret and analyze the hidden political structures of the communities in which he lives.

Central to the book is visual art, the previously mentioned fresco, forever in the process of revision, and which might reveal something of the truth if one knew how to interpret it—but even this is subject to transformation and internecine meddling, with the rival factions perhaps influencing what actually gets painted. The notion of the occult, an idea never too far from Klossowski's mind, is tied to the idea that something can be revealed and hidden at the same time: an occult truth reveals itself to those who are prepared to see it, but remains illegible to those who are not. What I find remarkable about *The Suspended Vocation* is that it is a fiction that has the function of an occult text with an absent center. It is a book caught up in interpretation, in the struggle to understand, but also in the frustration of things that escape understanding, the frustration of the struggle to know what is real and what is feigned. Even if the fictive novel that is the subject of the "real" review that makes up Klossowski's novel might try to provide a climax that wraps everything up, the reviewer is intent on picking that ending apart, on reminding us of all that is not said in it. Klossowski refuses a neat resolution and, in this challenging but ultimately rewarding novel, makes us think carefully and intensely about the way in which everything stable and substantive around us, the more and more we analyze it, threatens to reveal itself as made of cardboard.

—Brian Evenson

Brian Evenson is the author of over a dozen works of fiction, most recently *Song for the Unraveling of the World*. He lives in Los Angeles and teaches at CalArts.

THE SUSPENDED VOCATION

Under the title *The Suspended Vocation*, with no author listed, released in 194– by "Bethaven" in an edition of one hundred, of which we were able to locate only a single copy in Lausanne, there was published a narrative that at first glance would appear to be no different than any of the other so-called *Entwicklungsromans* that have been turned out by Protestant or Catholic authors. Although written in the third person, the book might well be taken as a fictionalized autobiography, a confession of the author's various religious experiences. Nevertheless, as we shall demonstrate below, it would not be incorrect to consider the book a sort of dual biography: not, strictly speaking, the story of one man's conversion, but rather the story of a vocation, and the ways in which this vocation was subsequently called into question by Providence. Indeed, as is so often the case in this genre, Providence and the author seem consistently at odds—even though, if we may venture our opinion, art would seem to consist rather in following Providence's lead, for if God works in mysterious ways, ordering our lives, how much more unbelievable must these ways seem at secondhand, to the reader, and how many mortal novelists truly manage to surprise and convince all at once? Admittedly, this is a strictly literary perspective, but let us not forget that since the tradition of the religious novel began here in France—leaving aside the medieval didactic tradition, mind you—the truly great practitioners in the genre, from Barbey d'Aurevilly to Léon Bloy and Georges Bernanos, have all been apologists as well as novelists. (Greater apologists, perhaps, than artists? But that's a question for another time.) Of course there are many so-called "thesis novels" in the world, but is there such a thing as a religious thesis novel whose only proposition is the demonstration of the experience of faith? Doesn't this require much more than a mere demonstration of aesthetic mastery, and wouldn't authenticity of experience be the most immediate way to set the reader on the road to Damascus? Take Bloy for example; it is, all in all, the tenor of his daily life that is communicated to the reader of his novels, to the reader of his journals too: it is his anger, his fits of rage—preludes and epilogues to his more numinous moments—that truly speak to us, that attract and repel the reader. (After all, nothing is more communicable than rage, nothing so productively irritating as the pathos of anger and the invective it inspires. Whether it's prophetic by nature, or, on the contrary, wholly irreligious, anger is always a good way of getting someone's attention, and nothing puts a reader so much at ease as being rebuked. There is of course a whole rhetorical tradition founded upon rage, utilized by preachers since time immemorial and inspired by the prophetic pedagogy of scripture, a tradition that, in turn, thanks to the orators of the French Revolution, found itself transformed from that purely oratorical mode into a literary genre, which, married to a certain sort of delirium, allowed a whole new range of temperaments to share their ill humor with the world, as others do their good; and it little matters whether this ill humor, these qualms, these rages were provoked by bourgeois stupidity (Baudelaire and Flaubert); by the utilitarianism and moralism of capitalist society (Breton, the surrealists); by positivist atheism (Barbey, Villiers de l'Isle-Adam); or, finally, by the cult of the "right-minded" (Bernanos).)

For whom does a religious novelist really write? For atheists as much as for the faithful flock? Primarily, we say, for the reader of novels: a reader who, upon opening the book in question, is ready to suspend his disbelief in whatever may transpire for the characters in the story, up to and including miracles and the necessity for martyrdom, simply because he has, for the time being, accepted the universe of the novel, by virtue of having taken the time to read it, and with it has accepted the reality of the novel as being one of faith, this being one of the rules of the game he has thereby agreed to play; all this leading to little in the way of consequences, save perhaps for the reader's verdict upon the book, upon himself, and, above all, upon the life he is currently living. If such insignificant notions are all that are at stake, we might as well—and do pardon us for the comparison—read pornography. (Which is not to say that all powerful reading experiences don't have an influence, of one sort or another, upon the free will of the reader. One does not read with impunity, and to consent to a fictional reality means precisely to experience this fiction along with reality.) If, on the other hand, the reader *is* a believer, he knows he is in any case meant to believe nothing while he reads, that he is meant to approach the work in a "spirit of disbelief," because he is aware that, even if the author is on his side, both reader and writer must remain ever vigilant, out of the corners of their eyes, for "whomever does *not* believe," that third person to whom everything is in fact addressed, the eternal atheist, eternally unconvertible, standing always between author and reader, whose presence is only magnified by his fundamental lack of devotion toward this undertaking of which he does not approve, an interpretation that he would like to deny; and yet it can be said that it is the very presence of this disbelief that increases the intensity of works predicated upon faith, for—if the author knows his business—he will thwart the intrusions of this invader, will beat it back inch by inch, forcing it to give ground, finally hounding it back to its lair inside the reader himself, where this pernicious atheist has been slumbering all along. This isn't so different, in fact, from what one finds in those combative freethinking novels that no longer seek to prove the hollowness of all religious dogma—a question that, for such authors, has already been entirely settled—but rather humanity's ineptitude in finding practical uses for such beliefs in its daily existence. There are two chief ways of making this argument: the first and already somewhat hackneyed method is to show up the practice of religion as little more than a hoax, the demonstration of which point seeks to goad the reader's sense of fairness into open revolt—after, say, the plots of this or that sinister priest are revealed for what they truly are, under the most tragic circumstances possible, for example a scenario featuring these fraudulent traditions being upheld at the cost of a human life; the second, more modern way, which would seem to pose far more serious a threat to the literature of faith, is for atheistic novelists to portray characters who, despite being nonbelievers, perform good works and acts of charity and even suffer martyrdom, the better to establish that good works can be undertaken precisely because one is under *no* supernatural obligation—according to these novelists—to do so. In these books, believers are introduced not to play the role of foil, as are the godless characters in religious novels, but more to embody that same invisible sense of skepticism we've already mentioned as haunting all novels of faith. And yet, strange to say, rather than finding this latter trend troubling, Christian literature, were it more aware of its position, would see instead that it has everything to gain from it; for, having arrived at this sort of argument, the literature of atheism has saddled itself with the goal of setting a morality without God against the amorality of belief, thus making itself vulnerable to self-criticism, since art can't long survive in an atmosphere of pure and simple morality—not without falling into the most vulgar pragmatism. Moreover, if morality is just another arbitrary rule in the game of life, in what sense, now, is it any more legitimate than aesthetics? Where, if we have reached this point, is the seriousness of existence? And what to do, then, with the accusations of immorality levied against religion and its own literary propaganda? (Lest we find ourselves vowing to bring about the destruction of all art the better to finally save humanity . . . Or else find ourselves defending this irreducible form of human expression to the extent of separating it from any actual demonstration of its qualities. For the artist—if the art one produces is truly spurred by an inner necessity—always demonstrates and substantiates the existence of a reality above not only aesthetics but morality as well, and cannot help but testify to a life superior to life. All ideological literature, as we know too well, seeks only to provoke action, and in so doing to prolong the immediate experience of *this* life; it doesn't even pretend to try to give us access—like any literature worthy of the name—to a new order of experience, spiritually speaking: one belonging first to the author, but then transmitted to and taken up by the reader in turn . . . Though Eliot is on record as insisting that in modern readers this capacity—this willingness to follow authors into whatever discoveries they might have turned up in their work— has gradually diminished in favor of reading solely to relive their own raw experiences, to find in literature confirmation of whatever it is they already believe, thereby preventing themselves from passing into this other reality, thereby barring themselves from entering the Promised Land in which all authentic creation is to be found.) To this we say: certainly the Christian novelist is immoral; he is gladly so, if morality is, as these atheistic, moralizing or demoralizing novels claim, nothing more than the heroism of a tightrope walker dangling above a void—the heroism of the dangling man—then how could a religious writer give any credence to an existence sanctified by a mere balancing act? But the Christian novelist can only benefit from being surrounded by his adversaries: he will learn much from witnessing their "fighting techniques," and a close attention to atheistic moralizing literature may yet warn him away from utilizing the patronizing propaganda of self-improvement, which methodology he ought to abandon, and gratefully, to his enemy. Moreover, the example of demoralizing literature serves only to provide further grist for the Christian novelist's mill, in that it furnishes him with more and better tools with which to make his own case. For example, has the abuse of supernatural tropes—so derisory and so sterile—in religious literature not now found its effective counterpart in the atheistic novel's abuse of sordidness and abjection (and not only by the existentialists!)? If the one and only concern of a Christian novelist is the "diminution of the traces of original sin," and consequently an approach to holiness (if admittedly a holiness following from a single and unique example), that Christian author must nonetheless never forget that he who has resigned himself to write—because substituting for action an inability to refrain from setting his own self in high judgment—is he who resides at the farthest extreme from the very sainthood he has spent his life envisioning. And because a religious writer can hardly be a hagiographer of imaginary saints, and because there's nothing quite so presumptuous as to speak of grace as if it were already granted, his task will be to show the reader what it really means when we are told that grace has been denied us. Much as it would be necessarily perfidious to put into practice the proverb that where sin abounds, grace abounds much more, so too it would be nothing less than gratuitous to describe a fictional superabundance of grace in our actual abundance of sin. A Sartre, a Camus—they must be directors of conscience, since they are attempting to chisel themselves a Decalogue that will be all the more commendable to accept in that it will be all the more permissible to reject. But the Christian novelist will never be a director of conscience: he is the opposite of the priest, since everything that a priest learns under the seal of the confessional, the novelist makes it his business to publicize. To the confessor it falls to scrutinize, to unravel the Lord's mysterious ways; to the novelist it falls to avoid confusing these ways with his own petty contrivances. The novelist's role, I dare say, is akin to that of the false prophet of Bethel, who led astray the man of God from Judah, but who nonetheless, through his lie, carried out the will of God upon His chosen. When a Christian novelist says, humbly, "I am no more than an ineffective drudge," this is simply another brand of hypocrisy: if he really believed this, he wouldn't waste all his time with books, but get himself to a monastery with all deliberate speed. But when a Christian novelist recognizes that he is a false prophet, recognizes that all he says of the kingdom of heaven is a counterfeit that must nevertheless and consistently appeal to the most carnal appetites of his readers in order to put them into the ideal state to receive a taste of holiness—since it is not for him to give them the thing itself—and when he recognizes that he can only ever distract them with his fripperies, he will at least have the merit of remaining conscious of the mechanisms of his trade, which consists much more of thwarting the Lord and His mysterious ways than of successfully conceiving them.

* * *

To return at last to *The Suspended Vocation*, we have to wonder if the author of this novel ever took the trouble to think these difficult issues through. Perhaps we are only projecting these questions onto him? Or perhaps he did at least touch on them in the writing of his story, since it was of course the pretext for the above digression—but if this was the case, he certainly didn't arrive at any solutions. No doubt he too was searching for a new technique; no doubt he had to settle for trial and error. But we must recognize at least one of the author's techniques as being somewhat interesting: his insistence upon addressing all issues of a supernatural order by suppressing every nuance in his text that might have evoked things not of this world. An outright unbeliever couldn't have done better if he'd set out to describe, in the spirit of denigration so fashionable today, this same group of characters, all of whom nonetheless belong to the religious life. Was this intentional, or did the author badly bungle the execution of his subject? As yet we cannot say, and so we must content ourselves with pointing out the strange effect generated here by what might otherwise be taken for a "documentary" novel. Granting for the time being that the author did indeed set out to give us just this impression, we note that he has provided more a series of psychological portraits in his novel rather than anything resembling a cast of successfully imagined characters, to the point that the reader must wonder whether the somewhat static nature of these figures is the result of a pure and simple transcription of lived reality. Transcription and not transposition, since if our author lacked artistry, he was fully furnished with the art of observation—yet this observer remained perhaps too close to and interested in his models to be able to properly digest them, break them down, and reconstitute them, breathing life into them with the imaginative force of genuine talent. It's easy enough for us to believe that insofar as the real events recounted in the novel must have been lived in close contact with these characters, the personages in question became so vital to the development of the hero's inner life that the author was unable to sufficiently "objectify" them by changing any details of the events to which this very novel ought to have put a full stop, on which this tale should have been the final word. Could it have been to overcome these disadvantages, born of the author's own inadequacies—mind you, this is only conjectural, but could as easily be seen as evidence of the author's cleverness in overcoming his own novelistic shortcomings—that he tells his story entirely through a series of bluntly described external events, which on the other hand combine to form a tale of great strangeness?

To get down to the details: This story of a defrocked seminarian takes place against a backdrop of social upheavals in which we are no doubt meant to recognize the dark years from which we as a nation have ourselves just emerged. The darkness of those years is rightly described here as devolving from an ideological conflict, though whether the author means to reference the war of the Third Reich against the world's democracies, or rather a completely different sort of battle, taking place on an exclusively spiritual plane, is by no means clear. Sometimes it would seem that we are meant to think of the Nazi occupation of France, with its troops, its police, its torturers, as when we are told of the depredations suffered by both religious and civil society at the hands of the mysterious "Black Party." At other times, it would seem, on the contrary, that this same organization is merely the Inquisitorial arm of the Church, and that the author—rather surprisingly, since the clearest thing about his novel is that it is an apologia for the spirit of holy obedience—has borrowed for its sobriquet an old anticlerical term for the ultra-rightist, so-called "Priestly Party." Even still, the operations of this Inquisition are not strictly spiritual; according to whispered colloquies in the cloisters, we are told, the Inquisition contains within itself a kind of third order licensed to use physical restraint (that is, violence)—much like sanatoriums, putatively no more than places of detention for "medical consultations," yet well prepared for when these consultations end with the inevitable and permanent sequestration of their "patients"—and able to deploy an army of theological informers in the persons of zealous novices who, having earned the confidence of certain of their superiors, denounce to their Novice-Masters the least hint of doctrinal innovation among their peers. From this we can see that the author is less interested in retracing recent history than in depicting an otherwise unlikely, not to say anachronistic, situation in which a religious order (never explicitly named) able to exercise spiritual terror within the Church vies with a rival order over the question of methods—for, as we shall see, it's all a matter of fighting certain secular initiatives taken in tandem with certain religious orders, and their opposition by a secular clergy loyal to the extant Church hierarchy (which is to say, in the end, a conflict between two different authorities)—and, consequently, a religious order whose particular mission is to hound to its last redoubt a community of devotees at risk of forming an Invisible Church within the Church, much as the Church itself already constitutes a sort of Freemasonry within secular society. This "sect," which one of the characters considers far more formidable, properly speaking, than its persecutors—with innumerable and elusive members, it's like a serpent with coils everywhere, whose segments always reunite no matter how many times its enemies succeed in slicing it into two or three—has apparently given itself over to a folk ritual that the Inquisitors consider colossally suspect because it has no foundation in either tradition or dogma, and which its practitioners promulgate under the appellation "Our Lady of the White Marriage," more or less knowingly taking advantage of the resulting confusion with more customary Marian devotions in order to insinuate into their worship the sublimation of certain, let us say, "emotional conflicts" that can serve only to further compromise spiritualization and the only ceremony accepted by convention. But before we continue with these details, let us first pause to examine this notion of persecution: a persecution in which the hero of *The Suspended Vocation*, over the course of dealing with his own myriad perplexities, assists without ever deliberately taking part; a persecution he believes he must oppose, without, however, rallying absolutely to the side of the persecuted devotional community; a persecution he even adopts for himself, in the end, becoming his own tormentor when what he believes to be the Black Party loses control of the Inquisition. The theme of persecution brings us back again to the war years: Did recent historical events—for example the Nazi persecution of the Jews—suggest to the author this peculiar vision of life within the Church? A conclusion difficult to avoid, given that during our hero Jérôme's peregrinations through what he calls, using the same terminology employed by both the Black Party and the Devotion, the "occupied" Church (Hitler's occupation obviously serving here as a metaphor)—during his travels from one monastery to another, from seminary to seminary, in search of superiors who can "understand his views on the mission of the Church in a world of civil wars"—he runs up against what are termed "demarcation lines" established by the Black Party (bringing to mind, of course, the borders delineating occupied Paris from "free" France during the war), in this case simply made up of houses of worship tasked with intercepting any possible messengers sent by the Devotion, themselves tasked with crossing these lines in order to insinuate themselves into the sympathetic houses beyond. Toward the end of the book, the Inquisitorial

Party is relieved of its duties by another, infinitely more tolerant faction, whose tolerance—Jérôme laments—will allow the Devotional community to prevail absolutely, and this contributes, apparently, to his "suspending" his "vocation." It is surely to be understood, however, that the true import of all these lucubrations—which serve, after all, as the backdrop to a rather obscure psychological drama—is their use as a veil behind which the author can disguise actual internecine conflicts that he prefers to indict via implication rather than denounce in plain language. No doubt the author would have us believe it is solely due to his *hero's* crisis of faith that our injudicious protagonist has taken to projecting his own spiritual torments onto these contemporary convulsions within the religion to which he thought himself called, aspiring to fight evil "from the ramparts of the Church, that besieged citadel"; but instead of picking a side, "instead of taking part resolutely in the sallies of the Inquisition, or else waiting in silence for the hour of their attack, as obedience would have demanded," Jérôme is seduced by the contemplation of these rumors of internal strife, which so strangely correspond to his own perpetual state of inner conflict, and thus, distracted from the real struggle, he gives himself up to "those dissensions that never disrupt the Holy City with the same intensity as they do hearts deprived of peace." As far as Jérôme's unfortunate imagination goes, the Devotion must be none other than the "vast brotherhood of Sodomites" concealed by the Church, and here we should note that it is by no means out of the question that the author is referring—via the substitution of one category of persecuted persons for another—to the undeniable connection, in this context, between anti-Semitism and homosexuality. We know first of all that whenever a scapegoat is needed for secular purposes, the powers that be have long since sought to exploit the anathema that hangs over the Jews, and that, if the persecution of the Jews was stage one of Nazism, it soon managed to kill two birds with one stone and reach Christianity as well by undermining the Semitic origins of the Church; secondly, we know too that despite the profoundly homoerotic nature of Nazism, the accusation of harboring homosexuals served in its turn as a defamation leveled against all religions resisting Hitler in Germany. Yes, anti-Semitism is necessarily homoerotic, and the parallels between homosexuality and Nazism are quite clear: on the one hand, in anti-Semitism, the deeply ambivalent relationship between victim and tormentor; on the other, with the invert, the relationship between active and passive participants. In addition, there is a whole body of literature that attests to the secret attraction as well as repulsion exercised by the finesse and so-called effeminate temperament of the Jew upon men possessed of a hidden sodomitical streak. And, lastly, we know of course the terrible proscription placed on homosexuality by the Judeo-Christian faiths, finally and most definitively from the mouth of the Apostle Paul. In this respect, one could conceivably look upon the Nazi-homosexual axis—in its persecution of first the Jews and then the Church, in its pretense to have established a new world order of wholly masculine and virile sentiments—as a form of spasmodic vengeance wielded by that ancient idolatry of man by man, and surely not for the last time, against the matriarchal values that the Church has maintained despite the vicissitudes of centuries. Not, mind you, that the author ever names the Nazis or the Jews: presumably he thought that putting the facts to his readers too baldly would attenuate the purely literary qualities of his allusive fable, which, as we've noted, is mainly concerned with portraying his protagonist's various struggles with reality. Moreover, what he wants to make understood is that insofar as this reality is reflected in the mind of his protagonist, it is reflected in reverse: the need to designate a guilty party persists, but the very one who wanted to take up the lash is targeted, only to be excluded in turn as an object worthy of persecution. The fact that the author may himself have belonged to the initial party of "persecutors," and is now seeking in his writing to reverse the roles of victim and tormentor after his obligatory mea culpa, might explain why so few copies of his "account" were published in Lausanne. All the more reason to underscore here the relationship between the author and the hero of his story: the protagonist is not, or not necessarily, in our reading, a self-portrait. At times we are even forced to give credence to the author's own contention (at the end of his book) that he was merely an observer standing as witness to his protagonist's struggles—that he (the author) sought in vain to influence him (the hero), and that the hero, after a long debate with the author—a debate the latter presumed he had won—reacted negatively to the author's obscure advances. Thus, between the man we believe to be the author and the man the author made into his character, the relationship resembles less that of an artist to his self-portrait than that *resentment* which springs up between two men who, misled by similarities of character, come to believe that they can unite to act in apparent concert, but are in fact brought together by the secret intention of the one to enslave the other. In the end, the first of them (the hero) slips away and the second (the author) vows eternal hatred for the first . . .

But we mustn't insist on this reading. The essential point is that we are at the beginnings, here, of a "system of protest" first glimpsed in our hero Jérôme's conversation with one of the Fathers of the monastery where he's begun his novitiate. This Father will put what Jérôme has felt only confusedly into categorical terms. Jérôme, meanwhile, believes he is being singled out for abuse, because the Father, addressing him in a monologue, never giving Jérôme a chance to explain himself, seems to have taken him for an apostate when in fact he is preaching to a wholehearted convert. Jérôme had spoken to him of Nietzsche's final illness and the links to the image of Christ in Nietzsche's life and works. But at the mere mention of the solitary philosopher of Sils Maria, the Father becomes enraged; he sums up his horror with these words: "Such *excessive virility* is nothing less than a cancer that must be excised!" What he calls *excessive virility* is what, to his mind, is most immediately responsible for our civilization of forges and factories, which, aligned with "this plague of virile values denatures, demoralizes, and degrades! Those who want to dominate," says the Father, "want industry, those who want industry want a proletariat, and those who want a proletariat will bring about the eradication and devastation of the countryside, the destruction of entire households, nothing but distress and revolt! And those who bring about the revolt of the masses must want the inevitable repression to follow. Yes, this excessive virility that has been unleashed upon the world and threatens the spiritual Matriarchy of the Church—much as the Dragon threatens the Woman of the Apocalypse—has found, in the modes of production to which it leads and the social convulsions they cause in turn, its own vicious circle: *the regime of the social penitentiary is its latest creation, and torture chambers are the final word of these so-called virile values—and, after all, the relationship between suspect and informer, torturer and victim, is the secret basis of sodomy.*" When Jérôme reports these words to his Novice-Master, the latter denies that the Father ever could have concluded his lecture in such terms. Jérôme swears he is acting in good faith and that he would never twist the Father's words. To which the Novice-Master replies, "You added that last bit yourself!" And since it's out of the question for Jérôme to return to his reverend interlocutor to ask for confirmation—a novice must not betray the trust a Father has placed in him—Jérôme accepts the Novice-Master's interpretation and winds up believing that the last few words must indeed have been his own invention. And the author seems to hold the same opinion.

Jérôme will admit later that he himself escaped from the sin of sodomy only by falling into that of adultery, finding therein a life so suited to him that it ended up worsening his innate passivity, his utter lack of initiative in life—another sin, and one that is its own punishment. He isn't freed from this lassitude until the day he discovers that he's been replaced, betrayed in turn by the adulteress in question; he then finds he is possessed of singular abilities as a mediator, because he's the one who winds up bringing the faithless wife back to the fold, as it were, reuniting her with her husband and continuing his friendship with both halves of the married couple—his empty scruples never allowed him to imagine being the cause of a final rift between them!—while on the other hand attaching himself to the very man he believes to be his new rival, simply on account of this fourth party having supposedly sullied Jérôme's mistress. Now, too, it seems that the very fact of the woman's additional betrayal serves as her primary attraction in Jérôme's eyes. Moreover, his newfound fascination with the defilement of the women he loves happens to be complemented by their propensity to betray him. From his own temptation to do evil, leavened by the irresolution preventing him from actually accomplishing much of it himself, and, as a result, from his perpetual penchant for bringing in additional participants so as to enjoy the pleasure of seeing evil nonetheless consummated, there is only one power that can extricate him: the Body of Christ, which absorbs all perversities. Jérôme has barely returned to the practice of the sacraments when the need not only to share them, but also to administer them to others, overmasters his desire to see evil done. The author would like to help us to understand the inseparability of these two needs in his hero, but in seemingly obeying the rule that we perceive our writer to have set for himself—that is, to indicate the presence of the supernatural only through the absence of any manifest supernatural phenomena—he risks committing the opposite error and so reducing his novel to little more than a psychological commentary on religious life. Can one speak of demoniacal forces without naming them? The author states categorically that they have no name; but isn't it precisely in dealing with such nameless horrors that one departs the sacramental sphere of confession and enters the clinical sphere of psychoanalysis? After all, isn't one of the most important stages of Jérôme's progress his visit with Persienne, the so-called "euthanasic" priest, and doesn't the author present this meeting to us as one of the seminarian's mistakes? Yes, the fact that our hero *wants* to battle demons, that he seeks to identify them using the Book of Revelation as his guide, and yet wants still to come to grips with these forces in much the way an alienist might probe the dark reaches of the mind—we can certainly take this seeming paradox as not only a defining characteristic of Jérôme, but a symptom of his ongoing crisis. Yet this feint only increases the peril for our author, who as a result treads dangerously close to psychobabble rather than offering a clear and straightforward description of the machinations of the Evil One, thus making a fool of himself with his prohibition against the supernatural before going right on to try to make a fool of his reader.

As far as the plot goes, however, Jérôme's struggle against his own memories, and the thoughts this struggle elicits in him, mean that, while he's a novice in a monastery supposedly controlled by the Black Party, he winds up colliding with a certain nun of great influence known as Mother Angélique, treating her as if she were a personal enemy and, judging that her doctrine—based upon a rigorous distinction between the *natural order* and the *order of grace*—will serve only to compromise the cause of their Party. Even though the monks of this monastery recognize the urgency of the Inquisition, they nonetheless harbor those whom the Inquisitorial Party is pursuing, because Mother Angélique's doctrine has made them disapprove of "black" methods. Jérôme has no desire to associate with the *persecuted*, but he can do nothing about the fact that he is now being treated as a *suspect* of the Inquisition. Jérôme thus feels obligated to take the methods of the Black Party even further, since in his eyes they alone among his colleagues seem to have some practical experience fighting the forces of darkness.

To return to the opening section of the novel, when Jérôme claims to his Novice-Master that he's developed a proof that the whole of our so-called *natural order* is an illusion, however clever, fabricated by demons, his Novice-Master suspects him of Jansenism, or, worse, Calvinism, and at this point Jérôme quits the novitiate, seemingly with the intention of heading to a seminary where his superiors might be more "understanding" of him—if for no other reason than that some adepts of the Devotion have made contact with him and suggested the move. Why not feel out the terrain? At this stage Jérôme knows the Devotion only from a distance and is ignorant of that sect's various mysteries. Though he has close friends "on the inside," information is scarce: only snatches of intelligence, scattered warnings, and occasional invitations (sent by La Montagne, fabled organizer of the resistance seeking to undermine the Black Party) are able to cross from "one zone to the other"—again the historic situation overlaps with the spiritual! Jérôme initially agrees to write secret reports for his new hosts on the activities of the Black Party, but just when he's left the monastery and thinks he's regained his freedom, as he's preparing to enter the seminary, he is pulled back in thanks to the invitation of a monk of the same order to which Jérôme previously belonged, but in another district, a monk who attributes the novice's failure to the naïveté of his Novice-Master, and offers to take him into the monastery of his own province for a year of contemplation and further study. It is here, in this new monastery, that the strange episode of the fresco takes place. There is a painter here who has been working on a fresco in the apse of the sanctuary without ever being able to finish it. So many figures are roughed in—some more advanced in their execution, superimposed over others that the painter seems to have neglected—that Jérôme can't quite determine what scene they are meant to depict. The Virgin is clearly present, yet she appears in several different aspects: the left side of the fresco features what must be a representation of the *Coronation of the Virgin* by angels, while at her feet are gathered an eager group of Doctors of the Church, some of whom are in disputation—Jérôme thinks these must be the ones who denied the dogma of the Immaculate Conception—while others are prostrate in adoration before the revealed mystery. In the center of the fresco, we see the Virgin appearing to Saint Bernadette, representing the confirmation and triumph of the Marian Dogma. The right part of the fresco, as compared to the first two thirds, appears more or less empty and indicates some hesitation on the part of the artist: it is barely filled in with the outlines of two figures, one in a kneeling position, arms raised toward Bernadette's vision and so stretched likewise above the other figure, who is lying down.

What makes this second figure all the more striking is that its head, against the background—which remains white—appears to be the most *realized* part of the entire fresco. It is the face of a young woman, her mouth partly open, her eyes in ecstasy before the vision. While this last detail is handled very realistically, elsewhere in the picture Jérôme observes a mixture of two rather different approaches. The entire fresco is dominated by the contrast between the colors green and red. Jérôme learns that the painter is not one of the Fathers, but a Lay Brother. At least in this monastery, the Lay Brothers tend to represent a subversive element. Since they're tasked only with manual and domestic work in the community, according to the Rule of the Order, Jérôme would have ventured to speak of a form of class struggle to explain the tension in the monastery, had he not been informed after a few days that there are devotees of "Our Lady of the White Marriage" among them: men of obscure backgrounds, laymen that the Inquisition had sent away on a retreat, for reeducation—reeducation of their souls, so to speak—but who, according to Jérôme, demonstrating such a marked humility, such a need to carry out the hardest and most repugnant work available, joined the Lay Brothers here and early on spread the Devotion among them. This is what the old painter reveals to Jérôme when he admits that the execution of the fresco has been a continual source of problems for him. Among the Doctors at the Virgin's feet, he made the rather careless choice to represent those who had fought the Dogma as being prejudicial to the Holy Spirit; that is, Saint Bernard and Saint Thomas. Then, on the insistence of a certain ailing Father of the monastery, who died before Jérôme's arrival, the artist agreed, not without compunction, to repaint these two Doctors *with their faces veiled*. Since this part of the fresco was in the shadow thrown by the curve of the apse, he hoped at least to sketch in these figures without alerting the community—if for no other reason than to ensure his work was finished before a public viewing. But his reworkings might possibly become visible during the office of Vespers; when Vespers are solemn, the altar is illuminated by a greater number of candles, shining more light on the sanctuary. The Fathers seated in the part of the choir facing this part of the apse could then easily see the two veiled figures, but perhaps they would also suppose that the painter was only touching up their features. Eventually, however, this would surely attract attention—perhaps because these other Fathers were already aware of the influence of the sick Father on the Painter Brother? When one or another of the monks came to pray in the choir, they did not interrupt the painter's work; however, banal circumstance soon led a Lay Brother to place a strong light bulb in a fixture heretofore unused, and right above the altered fresco. The Bursar Father came over for a look—not to check on the fresco's progress, but only to see the light fixture in use, which placed him right in front of the part of the composition representing the *veiled Doctors*. He immediately informed the Prior, who asked the Brother for an explanation. The old painter, despite the Prior's insistence, refused to impugn the memory of the deceased Father, and confessed only to a lack of judgment on his own part. On the orders of the Prior, he scraped away the veiled faces and, giving the Doctors their true faces, showed their features to be those of men conversing and asking questions. In any case, the Painter Brother notes to Jérôme, they will undoubtedly have to be entirely repainted; the Prior had brought to his attention the irreverent attitude he had given two of the most important theologians of the Church, their backs turned to the triumph of the Virgin, and his attempts to demonstrate that these Doctors were not assumed to "see" *the Dogma* that the crowning manifests and confirms were to no avail. At this point, Jérôme inquires of the painter how he plans to fill in the incomplete right portion of his fresco. The Painter Brother—in order not to betray himself?—indicates that he will simply show Pope Pius IX, who promulgated the Dogma, alongside the martyred Carmelite nun who had offered up her life for the Immaculate Conception. But Jérôme, ignoring the warning implicit in all that the Brother has just related, now wants to make the painter see the pictorial imbalance that will result from this plan: too many figures on the left of the Virgin and not enough weight on the right side of the image, even after the addition of a *Pius IX in contemplation next to the deathbed of the Carmelite who offered her life for the triumph of the Dogma*. Jérôme and the painter then look at his work more closely; what surprises and bothers Jérôme above all, he tells the Brother, is that the painter has represented the Virgin twice, already a fairly conventional fault in the composition (independent of any hieratic complaints); next, he shows him the extent to which the posture of the outlined figure of the Pope (who on this particular day is no longer kneeling, but sitting, leaning over) evokes affliction more than devotion, while the papal tiara, barely roughed out, in fact evokes the sort of solar crown usually depicted on the forehead of the Virgin Mary. "Don't you see that the figure you actually wanted to paint here, and who—appearing for a third time—might rescue the painting, is none other than *She Who Weeps*, Our Lady of La Salette?" As he speaks, Jérôme examines the perfectly completed head of the "Carmelite" up close, and he adds with much less assurance, "Look how harmoniously the two children to whom Our Lady of La Salette appeared, Mélanie and Maximin, would complete the composition!" But the painter is looking at Jérôme in stupefaction, and in a choked voice tells him, "*You're nothing but a provocateur!*" With that, he disappears. Jérôme has not yet realized his error; he will learn only later how trenchant and frightening his suggestion was for the painter. His first move is to hurry off to consult the monk who first brought him into the monastery; but the latter, as indicated by a note on his door, is away traveling, to Jérôme's great surprise. As our seminarian stands perplexed before the door of the cell, from down the long hallway, amid a din of clangs, chanting, and threatening cries, surges a crowd of Lay Brothers brandishing spades, scythes, chains, and incense-burners, some of them groaning and praying, others yelling curses. Jérôme is frightened by their numbers; it's impossible that all of them belong to the same community. In the lead they are shoving along the Bursar Father who, walking backward, is trying in vain to contain them, while Jérôme, hidden in the doorway, makes out the words "provocateur"—"Jesus Mary"—"Son of a Jew"—"Protect us from our enemies, Mary"—" . . . domite"—"Free us from this plague, Lord"—"Antichrist, nun's abortion!" "This way, this way," cries the Bursar Father, and as he directs them and the flow spreads to the nearly invisible far end of the hallway, Jérôme sees the Prior urging them on from behind, undoubtedly herding the mob into the next passage, waving his scapular mysteriously. This accomplished, the Prior approaches Jérôme, his face contorted: "My poor child, you don't know what you've done! The Lay Brothers now believe you're a Black Party spy! You know what that means—we can no longer keep you. Tomorrow, who knows, maybe even as soon as tonight, *they* might appear, and then I would be powerless to do anything but acquiesce." "*They*" are of course the Inquisitors, and so Jérôme, if he were indeed working for the Black Party, could hardly remain in the monastery without fear of falling prey, not to mere harassment—because what has just passed before Jérôme's eyes, what has just filled his ears, is, according to the author, "something else entirely"—but to the clandestine malevolence of the Lay Brothers (from which emanates this "something else entirely") that already sits at the heart of the disruption pervading the house. And then, even if he isn't, in fact, a member of the Black Party, should the Inquisitors become aware of his lapse, they could forever bar his entrance to any seminary, or even force him into a retreat among the Lay Brothers themselves, as a test—putting him at the mercy of their suspicions until he could find a way to convince them of his good faith, even making him participate in these strange "*processional swarms*" in which "no one knows how he will act, once he has been swept away." If Jérôme's conscience were clear, of course, he wouldn't back down for any reason, even if it meant confronting an official inquiry, for his soul would be at peace. But this absurd incident, which was itself perhaps meant only to test him—a trick he could have thwarted simply by standing firm—makes him lose his composure, not so much because he is guilty as because his pride has been wounded, as has his overly docile temperament. Here he begins to fall prey not to duplicity, per se, but certainly to the habitual bifurcation of the will we have already seen provoked in him by his own demons. Now, as he is returning to his cell, where he knows a monk saying his rosary is carefully keeping watch so that Jérôme can safely make his preparations for departure, he passes by the library, whereupon he comes to a realization that strikes him as more urgent still: he goes in to write a detailed report to La Montagne, leader of the anti–Black Party resistance, deciding there and then that he will be safest among the Fathers in the library, since it's been observed that the processional swarms tend not to invade this area. He spends a good hour in this manner, losing himself in writing out the details, no longer knowing whether he should present his discussion with the painter in front of the fresco as the cause of the "swarm" or rather present the fresco as a consequence of just such "swarms"—perhaps intended in the first place as a means of preventing these demonstrations. Finally, however, he decides to postpone finishing his missive. When he reaches his cell, he finds the Prior, the Provincial Father, and a Bishop conversing; kneeling and kissing the Prelate's ring, he has not yet risen when he hears, "We were just speaking very ill of the 'Inquisitor of Our Lady of the W.M.,'" from the Provincial Father, as the Prior and Bishop look on smiling. Disconcerted, Jérôme feels he has been caught, somehow, in the act of appealing to La Montagne, but before he has time to make excuses for himself, the Provincial Father asks him this question: "So, what do you think of the fresco?"—as if to help him regain his composure. Jérôme thinks he can answer to his own advantage: "It is repellant in many ways," he says.

"But," continues the Provincial Father, "didn't you say it could be perfected if only it included the appearance of *She Who Weeps*?"

"Yes, but for reasons of balance," says Jérôme.

"Balance," says the Prior. "Do you mean the balance of the

souls of this house?"

"Compositional balance," says Jérôme.

"Did you hear that, Monseigneur? I think we can leave the two of you alone"—at which point the Provincial Father and the Prior withdraw. As soon as they are gone, the Bishop takes Jérôme's hand and holds it in his, saying: "Really, this is indeed perfect, my son. You know, when I was still completing my studies, the seminarian subjected to the fresco test in this holy house had it much harder—at that time the fresco to be deciphered bore no emblem that could be so easily grasped by reference to one's own memory of an occurrence in the last century, such as the apparition of Our Lady of La Salette, and in those days the processional swarms were so frequent and so invasive that no one would have dared to step out of line to alert a neighboring Province or Diocese, or to denounce or accuse his teachers. It is not good, my son, it is not good for you to stay here. Have you been incardinated?"

"No, Excellency."

"Then I will adopt you and take you into my Diocese. You can pursue your theology far from all of these disputes. Before seeking out the enemies of the Church, fight them within yourself to better belong to Our Lord."

He then invites Jérôme to get into his car. At the wheel is not some ecclesiastical driver, but a nun. For the first time in this account, a woman appears upon the scene, and Jérôme is struck by the beauty of her features, which would seem hard were it not for the singularly tender look in her eyes. The Bishop introduces Jérôme to her, Mother Angélique, who belongs to one of the teaching orders. The Mother says she has known of Jérôme for a long time through their mutual "friend," La Montagne. But the introductions stop there and Mother Angélique drives the car: Where to? The author takes care to leave us in the dark as to the topography of this journey; like the monasteries and religious orders in his novel, the places through which the trio travels are never named. We understand simply that the episcopal car stops in a silent avenue of the capital or some other urban area. We have left the countryside for the city, we have left the "wilderness" for civilization, or at least we may assume so, and in the blink of an eye the author has moved our seminarian "from one zone to another": from one controlled by the Black Party to one held by the Devotion. On the day following Jérôme's arrival at Mother Angélique's convent, his Bishop decides he will stay with the Sisters before being placed in a presbytery: because of our seminarian's age—his is undoubtedly a late vocation—he will be allowed to dispense with seminary life. As this is a blatantly false pretext, the diocesan authorities must want an observer in Mother Angélique's house. All these circumstances conspire to give Jérôme a leading role in the very disputes he had thought to leave behind, and, as a result, a trap is laid for him: had he truly felt responsible for his vocation, his most pressing need would have been to follow the recommendations of his Bishop and concentrate on fighting the enemy within. But the latter doesn't press this point and disappears from the stage, for the time being.

"It ought to be known," says the author, who suddenly adopts a predicatory tone, "the extent to which the devil is capable of taking otherwise holy concepts and using them to manipulate us into maintaining the abjectness of our souls, giving us hope that we can make ourselves agreeable to God if only we succeed in savoring the sacred with as much gluttony as we enjoy the perverse. But it's pointless to change the object of our gluttony if that gluttony remains: heavenly provender can be savored only with the appetite of a new man. Such is the case with the characters we will now describe." In this second part of his novel, the author will show his hero caught in the crossfire of La Montagne and Mother Angélique. Yet we shall see La Montagne only through what Mother Angélique says of him, and the Mother through what La Montagne says of her. It isn't that the facts won't be reported to us, but that Jérôme will be unable to see them with his own eyes because he is in turn influenced by one and then the other. Thus the conflict over the fresco becomes, in retrospect, a projection of Jérôme's own internal conflict—just as the later episode of the "exhumation of the young nun" by the Spanish painter will bring to light the vilest elements of his soul, even as he feels himself drawn to the only truly innocent character in this account: Sister Théophile, who will bear the consequences of Jérôme's final exorcism.

Mother Angélique, presented as a woman of "majestic beauty"—she is said to be the great-granddaughter of the famous courtier Lauzun—is unfortunate enough to be possessed of an indomitable temperament: believing she has been victimized most unfairly by the situation that our so-called secular priests, who operate outside of the monastic life, have created for women in the Church, she can't help but see priests in an equivocal and even obsessional light. At times, when she sees priests being submissive, she imagines them as without will because they lack experience; at other times, when they show the slightest subtlety, she believes them ambitious and sly—and the only experience she'll allow that they might have accumulated she sees as wholly sinister. It's the same for her as for many women who enter the religious life on account of their sensibilities (and not because it makes any kind of sense): all these black-clad priests resemble nothing so much as "shady characters" forever sniffing around their nunneries. The author, taking Mother Angélique as she is when she meets Jérôme, only briefly fills in the woman's origins, the events in her life that could have determined or encouraged these delusions. It seems that during the initial conflict that pitted the Black Party against the Devotion and led to the "occupation" first of the parishes and then of the monasteries of various orders, whether by the adepts of the Devotion or by the "legions" or members of the Inquisitorial Party, Mother Angélique was given a rather daunting mission, which she carried off with a brio hardly to be suspected in persons accustomed to the contemplative life. Her superiors, and particularly a certain Father—the one that died before Jérôme's "test of the fresco"—apparently tasked her on behalf of the Church with directing a group of Tertiary Sisters intended, according to the author, to "neutralize the zones of the Black Party and the

Devotion both." Obedient only to the spirit of charity—"the sole form of obedience of which oversensitive natures are capable"—she apparently headed off the fanaticism of some, rescued others from persecution, and undoubtedly contributed to the Church's continued unity, as well as her own Order's coming into inquisitorial power. However, as much as monastic life seemed to satisfy the aspirations of her nature, her contact with the secular clergy apparently set off the disturbing reactions listed above, undoubtedly beginning during this mission; forced to grapple with her fixed notion that these priests were little more than "spies in black," she seems to have found herself in a state that her superiors couldn't have foreseen. By the time it's decided that Jérôme will be housed by Mother Angélique's community, her volatile state has worsened considerably.

Is it this obscure grievance that she bears with regard to the secular clergy that leads Mother Angélique to sympathize, at first, with La Montagne, who hopes to see a "regeneration" of the Church, not through the clergy itself, but through the devotional initiatives of a vast movement of laypeople (the likes of which we've already seen)? But soon Mother Angélique discovers, or thinks she discovers, in La Montagne something far more troubling than an ordinary "shady" priestliness: by all accounts, and despite his faith, La Montagne remains a member of that tribe scattered across the world thanks to the destruction by fire and brimstone of a certain notorious city . . .

"La Montagne didn't hide the fact that he had once counted himself among the numbers of that cursed tribe, which, like the Jews, seems to have survived by virtue of its own malediction," says the author. "Indeed, the most intransigent of his 'brethren' had never pardoned him for finally recognizing God's authority in passing the dread sentence that rained down sulfur and fire onto the cities of the plain at a time when the inhabitants' insolence threatened to put an end to the growth and proliferation of humankind." And yet, from the moment of his submission to the Church onward, La Montagne was suspected by his new confessors of being a double agent: Had he not, for many long years, and with such brilliance, extolled the "sovereign rights" of his "tribe"? Had he not demonstrated, in his own person, as much by the example of the many educational organizations he'd founded as by his audacious, scholarly reinterpretations of history, that this "tribe" had always served to prevent civil societies from lapsing back into the "darkness of matriarchal rule"? (Here the author seems to be answering or echoing the words of the monk conversing with Jérôme in part one.) Had he not described with eloquence and subtlety how the guidelines according to which his "tribe" behaves, by undermining the purely animal law that claims to ensure the conservation of society—even by encouraging its repression—had in fact bestowed upon humanity the structure and standards necessary for spiritual elevation? How could this earlier La Montagne, who in thought and deed never ceased setting the secret edicts of his brothers against the "barbaric law of the God of Jews and Christians," be the same man they now saw humble himself before that same "narrow and limited God"? The priestly La Montagne claimed to be horrified by both his "tribe" and the invisible seal with which it had marked him; and what was worse in the eyes of his ex-brethren, he went on to make that mark *visible*, bearing it like a stigma; he even came to feel that he had been *corrupted* by it.

"*Corrupt, yes, you are doubly corrupt now,*" the "ancients of this tribe" told him. "*Corrupted in our eyes by the God of the Jews, corrupted in your own eyes because you continue to belong to us, like it or not.* So be it! We shall be the 'demons' within you, since this is how you want it. *Let's see how well you manage to 'serve' us and 'He who casts out demons'* at one and the same time!" they added pointedly, with derision.

So, from that moment on, La Montagne—who according to the author had developed his talents as an educator with undeniable social success, founding schools, study groups, and "youth centers," and who, due to his philanthropic work to benefit juvenile delinquents, enjoyed general esteem in the most illustrious universities as well as among the most highly placed personalities of the judiciary in various Western capitals—found himself living a highly circumscribed life: a habitual night owl all but imprisoned in his grotesque villa. It's only now that he understands what it means to be a pariah, facing the rancor of the "ancients of his tribe" (among whose number the author of *The Suspended Vocation* might perhaps be counted) as well as the suspicions of his new ecclesiastical circle. The author speaks too of the *various ripples* that such a conversion must have stirred up in diocesan circles: some would have judged La Montagne's change of heart to be purely and simply the basis of a "Trojan horse" operation—might this paranoia be the origin, the reason for the founding of the so-called Black Party?—whereas others would have rejoiced at what they interpreted as being the first signs of the vast, forthcoming revolution of the lay piety against the secular clergy in a struggle for power. Indeed, once converted, La Montagne apparently showed particular zeal for the popular devotions; his creative talent also seems to have lent new and serious cohesion to the dispersed manifestations of Marian devotion. The author implies that the same scholarship which La Montagne had applied to the covert policy he nurtured with regard to his "tribe," and which he had so brilliantly developed in the cause of that "city" from which the vast community of his brethren take their name, was now put to work in service to the very devotion from which his faith had devolved. Without getting into details, the author wants to highlight the advantages for the Church of counting among its numbers a man whose long experience combines with an influence as robust as that of a Baden-Powel (*sic*). If the pragmatic expectations the author attributes to the Church truly existed—though naturally we must remind ourselves that we are dealing with a novel and not a history—they were, however, surely met with disappointment, due to the aforementioned conflict in La Montagne's soul. We shall see later that the partisans of Mother Angélique's doctrine will seek to attenuate and dispel this conflict, but that La Montagne, thanks to the particular circumstances of his conversion, categorically refuses. The author asserts his presumption that this character of his was led to conversion by a no doubt dubious series of circumstances—circumstances that should have made it possible "for those who wanted to channel and transform the devotional movement he'd initiated into a sort of scout troop" to foresee that this was a most serious error. Which is to say that our author imagines that his character La Montagne was converted by a *child*—and it is this, apparently, that he cannot "pardon"—much like the "ancients of the City of the Plains"—no more than he can pardon Jérôme for wanting to embrace the ecclesiastic condition to begin with. We can see that Anonymous was tempted here to reveal himself a little.

You see, the younger La Montagne had sacrificed his family fortune not only to his pet cause of youth education, but also to his other great passion. Noting that a love of sculpture and a taste for the monumental are known to be among the clearest and yet most discreet signs of the nostalgia this "tribe" always in "exile" bears for that "city reduced to ashes by a rain of fire and brimstone," the author informs us that La Montagne, previous to his conversion, had assembled a stunning collection of statuary. Even his famous villa, combining the neo-Gothic with modern styles, was purchased less for its comfort than for its monumental ugliness; this taste for the bizarre and grotesque being by no means the least of the manifestations of the "perversity" of its owner who, in those days, adopted the outmoded air of the aesthete and dandy. Having already reached a considerable age, La Montagne wore his gray hair long around his sculpted, noble features: deep-set eyes under a vast forehead, a large nose, and folds of disdain at the corners of his lips. "With his tall and beautiful body, almost always dressed in black, a cape upon his shoulders, his physiognomy evoked something spectral, aristocratic, and decadent, from which the slight suggestion of the clergyman was never absent."

Around this time, La Montagne had taken in a young cobbler's apprentice who had been dismissed by his masters due to symptoms of mental imbalance. This boy from Dauphiné, no older than fifteen, an orphan for whom his haberdasher aunt had been able to find a position in the capital, was a very sweet and charming child, but he frequently fell into a sort of torpor that he could escape only by embarking on a period of kleptomania. A juvenile court turned him over to La Montagne, who perhaps even thought of adopting him. The boy was taciturn, possibly intimidated by his benefactor, and couldn't bring himself to admit to La Montagne that he was involved with a band of thieves specializing in antiques, who themselves ran an antiques store on the side. The boy must have described his new, strange, sumptuous residence to his friends, and they must undoubtedly have planned to make off with some of the precious objects belonging to their little accomplice's guardian. One day, an older woman comes to La Montagne's home, presenting herself as an antiques dealer and seeking the sum owed to her by the master of the house for a group of statuettes that La Montagne allegedly sent his little "secretary" to acquire at her shop. La Montagne immediately suspects his young protégé of a breach of trust, but is surprised to hear that the boy's motivation might have been the acquisition of a work of art. Confronted with the old antiques dealer, the cobbler's apprentice has no choice but to admit to harboring the pieces in question, which he goes off to retrieve from his room. While La Montagne is kept in discussion with the supposed dealer, refusing to pay the price for these little statuettes, which are of no interest to him—they depict a woman sitting in front of two standing children, a boy and a girl—the gang goes to work in the other wing of the villa. When the old antiques dealer departs—at La Montagne's request, she leaves him the address of her store, which turns out to be false—La Montagne leads his charge into the hall where he keeps his own statues, the better to make the boy confess. As soon as they enter, however, La Montagne sees evidence that he's been burgled: one of his most beautiful antiquities, a crouching Eros of medium size, has been taken. In their haste to get away with the loot, the thieves also removed the tarp that had, for years, been covering a group of life-sized polychrome statues that La Montagne had purchased out of pure curiosity, unaware of their meaning; now he sees that the little statuettes he refused were merely miniature replicas of originals he already possessed, almost unbeknownst to him. A strange spectacle: unsuspected within this collection of statuary, amid this mute and petrified crowd of adolescent gods and ephebes—original pieces as well as ancient and Renaissance copies—was a seated woman richly but singularly dressed who, her face hidden in her hands, wept before two figures, a boy and a girl. "It's Our Lady of La Salette," says the boy, "and here are Mélanie and Maximin."

"Explain," says La Montagne, stupefied by this bizarre combination of burglary and folk religion. The child then admits his collusion, and in his confused confession to his guardian he mixes memories of his hometown with details of the theft: all that his haberdasher aunt had told him about the apparition of Mary at La Salette, where his aunt had taken him after his first communion . . . La Montagne is in less of a hurry now to press charges against the old antiques dealer than to tell his friends about the strange coincidence: without the presence of the young apprentice, no burglary; without the burglary—the theft of his crouching Eros—*She Who Weeps* would never have been identified. Knowing nothing about La Salette, he decides to go there with the boy. He will then be able to see the originals of the statue group he has owned for so long. Once there, the Father in charge of this important site shows La Montagne the different stations of *She Who Weeps*'s zigzagging itinerary. La Montagne returns convinced he has been visited by a *sign*. And it is this sign, as he interprets it, that brings about the great upheaval in his life, inside and out. He shaves his head; he dresses almost banally, making no special effort. His hobbies also change. He wants to start cooperatives to benefit the Marian Devotion and, for this reason, takes an interest in business. He divides his villa into two sorts of accommodation: the first for Marian devotees, and the other—consisting of the rooms at higher levels—for his retreats and meditation. From this point on, La Montagne's life too is split: his educational programs, his "youth centers," his rehabilitation projects—all of that is dead to him; yet it is now, when he seems the most dedicated to the monotony of business, that he most devotes himself to cases of young men gone astray—but only favoring those *chance* meetings in which he *wants* to see the workings of Providence. Thus does he develop his discipleship: the boys and men with whom he becomes involved are soon either his catechumens or his enemies. His proselytical ardor is equaled only by the curiosity that makes him gravitate toward these young souls in need of a cause to which they might be sacrificed. Hence too La Montagne's increasingly avid search for other contemporary Marian apparitions—that of La Salette remaining the crucial revelation since it was the one that turned him against himself. The discontinuity imposed by the very nature of his conversion is etched into La Montagne's character, releasing forces in him that, until then, had apparently been dormant within his appreciation of the beauties of the human body, frozen in inanimate stone. The violence of the shock he received from Our Lady resulted too in a new rhetorical violence he'd never previously been known to exhibit. Hence his taste for sharp contrasts, not least the contrast of his past with his present: his collection of statues bores him, but he will never sell it, will never remove *She Who Weeps* from its midst; on the contrary, he will add polychromes to the collection, and examples of contemporary religious folk art. Visions and interpretations of the End Times—the days of the Prophet Joel's prediction that the children of the world would themselves see visions and speak prophecies—are particularly choice, linked as they are to his old taste for cataclysm. Desperate situations for others, far from upsetting him, are quite attractive to La Montagne, and send him into ecstasies; they are for him just so many foretastes of the final desolation awaiting this world, and the more they occur, up to and including instances of outright iniquity and horror, the more likely supernatural intervention becomes. The attraction presented by young men, previously such serene visions to La Montagne, is now a source of both distress and consolation for him: for if, as his brethren reproached him, they have become his personal demons, donning the faces of boys to lead him astray, might it not also be the case—given the grace accorded to visionary children—that this very attraction is no more than a hidden form of La Montagne's own election to grace by the spirit of childhood? This is the uncertainty, the paradox that torments La Montagne at the heart of his conversion: he must aspire with all the more intensity to receive the spirit of grace residing in youth given that his attraction to boys is surely the work of Satan. La Montagne is thus hostile to any system of thought that might seek to probe the central mystery of his faith; he is horrified by Mother Angélique's disciples, who claim that nature and grace are distinct and opposed. The only arguments that could move him would be ones with a visceral, violent power, because only rage, crushing every inclination toward rational thought—which, besides, La Montagne believes is a tool of the demon, sent in order to trap us—can protect him against the insinuations of an interlocutor; only high drama of whatever sort can persuade or move him, for a dramatic turn of events—like the one that occurred in his own home—is always the promise of a miracle, and as such is the only hope that he might forget the demons that are devouring him.

* * *

As for Jérôme, Mother Angélique discerns his torments perfectly. They are not unlike her own. She takes pleasure in making an accomplice of this "future priest" of whom she surmises that his own intelligence poses the greatest threat to his vocation: incapable as he is of giving up independent thought, as the spirit of obedience dictates, how could Jérôme not welcome as solicitude and esteem all the notions that the Mother invents to sharpen his pride? Since everyone else expects him to demonstrate the self-sacrifice befitting the habit he's donned, he can only become more attached to this woman who knows how to nourish in him precisely what ought to die, and so she soon succeeds in further dividing him against himself. Having fallen into this degree of dependence, he winds up fearing nothing so much as seeming to fail in her eyes. When she catches Jérôme being troubled by his scruples, the Mother needs only to chastise him, saying, "I suppose you aren't up to this—but if you're not, you know you'll only ever be a doormat," and he's immediately afraid of becoming just that. And he will respond, sadly, "I disappoint you," incapable as he is of seeing the truth of even these first few steps under the Mother's control. And how easy it is for the Mother to dissuade Jérôme from finishing his report to La Montagne—it would be, she says, his second and undoubtedly final faux-pas; others wanted him to believe that he had passed the "fresco test," perhaps, but this "success" could just as well be judged a failure, because over here, she says, the Devotion runs *its own Inquisition* . . . "But," says Jérôme, "over there they thought I was a spy for the Black Party—here I only have to bring up the image of *She Who Weeps* and I'm called an 'inquisitor' for the Devotion! So I'm now both a Black Party agent provocateur and, no doubt, in the eyes of the Black Party, a double agent . . . ?"

"The Black Party? But, my dear seminarian, that's a bogey-man invented by La Montagne! Whereas the Devotion actually exists, here and now—very much so!"

She reveals that the people who inspired the current fresco—the fresco whose central enigma the Bishop told Jérôme was much more humane than the one posed in his youth—are none other than the aforementioned and now deceased Father, and Mother Angélique herself. Together with the Father, Mother Angélique was at the time agitating against rationalist speculation as practiced by the great theologians, hoping to show instead the triumph of pure faith in pictorial form. Then La Montagne became involved and recommended a painter with whom he later made a pilgrimage to La Salette—the old painter whom Jérôme met back at the monastery was merely this as-yet-unnamed artist's factotum. La Montagne's painter was apparently the one who had the idea of painting all the Doctors of the Church with their faces veiled—not only Saint Thomas and Saint Bernard—and then, larger than life, Mélanie and Maximin before a gigantic *She Who Weeps*. But this project had stalled. The Prior of the monastery had wanted nothing to do with veiled Doctors or that sort of representation of the Virgin, and neither for that matter did the now-deceased Father, nor Mother Angélique. A battle immediately developed around the idea of the veiled Doctors: La Montagne laid the blame not with his painter but with Mother Angélique, accusing her of having suggested this depiction of the theologians in order to sabotage his desired representation of *She Who Weeps*.

It can be seen in these passages that the idea of the incomplete fresco must have struck the author as a good way to capture the ferment of a certain milieu in which various opposing fervors and forms of faith act in direct competition—all of them presented as mutually exclusive, because each affirming a certain temperament. But this feint is too obvious, and makes the novel as inert as the fresco it describes, in fact depriving it of all the liveliness of an actual painting: an unhappy side effect forever looming over all writers whenever an abstract form like language is made to evoke a concrete art like painting in order to depict reality in a manner that writing considers beyond its reach. It's true of course that the novel under consideration is taken up with various aspects of religious life, that visual art is essential to that life, and that it thereby has a legitimate claim to inclusion in *The Suspended Vocation*—even being woven properly into the plot thanks to this business about the fresco: the same way, one might say, as the theater scenes are utilized in *Wilhelm Meister* (without, mind you, comparing the two novels in terms of quality). But, as in Goethe's novel, there's an incessant passage here from life to fiction and from fiction to a reality beyond life; the author apparently saw in his fresco material a means, perfectly suited to the atmosphere of his book, for showing the reader how representations of objects of faith (here in pictorial form) can turn those objects into pretexts for petty human squabbles that would not otherwise have manifested. What's not clear is what the author hoped to gain by this demonstration: the implication would seem to be that either said objects of faith are *only* ever pretexts, masks for the forces of darkness within us, or else, on the contrary, they are indeed divine realities, but realities that, as they reveal themselves to the base human soul, raise up demons in us that cast these objects in their own demoniacal light. Here the author touches on a knot of problems dating back to the first battles of ecclesiastical modernism, which haven't even begun to be untangled. On the one hand we have doctrinal revelation, and cases in which such revelation has been confirmed by image and apparition—as for example when the Virgin confirmed the dogma of the Immaculate Conception during her appearance at Lourdes to Bernadette, who was perfectly ignorant of theology. But it's something else entirely when we have, on the other hand, apparitions relating not to doctrine but to traditional devotions, issued in the form of private and particular revelations—such as the one at La Salette. In the latter circumstance, we may hope that the devotion thus confirmed by the apparition tends gradually to overcome and replace the imagery specific to its appearance within the tradition, leaving us with the option of saying that the vision was never intended as more than a conduit through which grace could do its long work upon the soul chosen to receive it; or else that it was simply a means of more widely promulgating the devotion it served to initiate. But here is where the difficulties begin, the suspicions, the polemics: when the image presented by an apparition isn't already a part of the tradition but seems instead to inaugurate a new condition in the economy of revelation itself—such as the vision of the Sacred Heart given to Marguerite Alacoque, which has by now colored nearly all Christology—this leads, inevitably, to an entirely novel understanding of the Redemption . . . such as that proclaimed by *She Who Weeps*, when she told Mélanie, *If my people will not submit, I shall be forced to let go the arm of my Son*. As a result, Jérôme, who is supported in this by the Bishop, his Spiritual Director, can't keep himself from asking whether, after the Son of God has appeased the anger of the Father, the Mother of Jesus is then obliged to intervene and appease the anger of the Son . . .

And so, because these are the sorts of problem with which a

theology student can't avoid wrestling—because he must, naturally, be a product of his pedagogical environment; because he will have taken them in by osmosis; because his studies necessitate a continuous clash with the beliefs of his fellows, especially when these are presented as expressions of sensibilities both deeply personal and utterly incontestable—the author of *The Suspended Vocation* figured that he would dramatize them with this fresco business. But while his symbolic framework is effective enough, enabling the characters to reveal whatever it is they're hiding—the roughed-out state of the fresco, with its superposition of figures, making it possible to render in a somewhat theatrical way considerations that otherwise would be interior and abstract—we find that the author nonetheless deemed this insufficient for his aims, because he winds up belaboring the fresco device to the point that it severs all ties with such elevated themes. Indeed, we are soon told that the figures of *the group around the Pope in contemplation* and *the Carmelite sister in her death agony* have an origin that isn't devotional in the least. If you look closely, Mother Angélique tells Jérôme, you will see that the features of the Sovereign Pontiff are not those of Pope Pius IX at all, but of someone you may meet here, and as for the Carmelite sister, the model for her was a *dead woman freshly buried and almost immediately exhumed.* As she says this, the Mother shows Jérôme a photograph of a scene of sacrilegious violence committed by Barcelona anarchists during the Spanish Civil War: he sees a young dead nun whom the insurgents removed from her coffin, shamefully painted with make-up, and whose breasts they had uncovered and slashed. As soon as Jérôme sees this picture, he recognizes it from the collection that his "former rival" Malagrida used to exhibit at every opportunity after he returned from the Civil War, where he had fought on the side of the anarchists.

Malagrida, a Spanish painter well known in avant-garde milieus, Jérôme's friend during his years of rebellion, and the one he suspected of stealing his old mistress, is probably only a bluffer. When Jérôme was still at the novitiate, Malagrida met La Montagne, who was immediately taken with him and could not prevent himself from trying to attract the Spaniard with Christian trivia, which Malagrida seemed to embrace given the religious themes he began to choose for his paintings. First he discreetly introduced the image of bread and wine in compositions whose atmosphere would otherwise have seemed most opposed to the presence of the Eucharist. Then the pieces of bread in his paintings multiplied until they were not only obvious but virtually obsessional, becoming or seeming to become a profession of the painter's faith in the Presence. Malagrida apparently admitted to La Montagne that during the Spanish Civil War he had taken part in profanations of churches, monasteries, and nuns. All of this was probably pure fabrication, but it led La Montagne to try to interest the painter in the Devotion. He brought the painter to La Salette and mistook for conversion what was, in Malagrida, merely curiosity and amusement. It was in this way that Malagrida agreed to compose the fresco and represent the Apparition at La Salette as Mother Angélique had described it to Jérôme; moreover, he wanted to demonstrate his humility and abnegation by working under the strictest anonymity. But the difficulties raised by the Prior then emerged, and Malagrida took advantage of this to modify the composition several times, which explains its roughed-out state when Jérôme saw the fresco. When La Montagne realized that Malagrida wasn't keeping up with the project—the composition the painter had sworn to complete back when they were together at La Salette—he confronted the Spaniard. This is when Malagrida, perhaps to throw the Black Party off his scent, perhaps under the influence of the Father who had been Mother Angélique's spiritual director, the one who had passed away before Jérôme's arrival at the monastery—though this strikes us as rather unlikely—apparently came up with the idea of representing the *Pope in contemplation before the Immaculate Conception, close to the deathbed of the Carmelite sister who had offered her life for the promulgation of the Dogma.* He found an old Lay Brother to help with the work, the one Jérôme had met, who was merely a craftsman and house painter but whose pictorial abilities were developed enough to be of use; in fact, inventing some pretext or other, Malagrida entrusted this artisan with his sketches and, entirely abandoning the fresco, disappeared from the monastery without a trace.

The character of Malagrida acts as a foil, if not a double, for Jérôme. He represents the seminarian's past, coming back to haunt him, while his work—the fresco—depicts the dogmatic and devotional conflicts in Jérôme's life; his own objects of faith, so to speak, painted by his own inner demon—for Malagrida is certainly that!—serving to mock Jérôme's secret sins. But instead of turning away once and for all from the pandemonium of the fresco and the circumstances around this unachievable and incompletable work, Jérôme, under the pretext of further nourishing his spiritual and theological experience, steps into the convolutions of a labyrinth from which Mother Angélique—who already has thoroughly misled even herself—eventually will deny him any escape. In the meantime, and like many others before him, particularly certain ex-members of the Black Party, Malagrida, at first unbeknownst to La Montagne as well as to Jérôme himself, is currently hiding in Mother Angélique's convent. This satisfies his need to continue to see, without being seen, La Montagne's niece, with whom he is in love, and who has donned the habit in Mother Angélique's convent under the name of Sister Vincent. So, one day, Jérôme comes face-to-face with his former rival. To overcome the first, highly disagreeable instant of surprise, the seminarian wants only to speak to the painter about his eucharistic canvases. Malagrida responds with sarcasm and pretends to complain of the obligation he is now under to keep himself hidden, together with the fact that he has no suitable studio in the convent, and is wasting his time among virgins. When the seminarian implies that he knows what happened between the painter and La Montagne, Malagrida, changing tack, begs Jérôme to help him obtain a meeting with Sister Vincent. But Jérôme first wants to elucidate the flagrant likeness between the physiognomy of the Carmelite sister in the fresco and the face of the nun in the photograph of the Barcelona sacrilege. Malagrida admits the photograph is a fake, taken during a "party" organized by a certain Doctor Carpocratès (another of Jérôme's cronies before he entered the orders). (It's worth noting here how the author—the one time he introduces an indecent fact from the real world at large into his fiction—is quick to imply that nothing of the sort occurred; he does this to better sustain the image of what *could* have occurred, because only the image that enters Jérôme's mind matters.) It seems this Carpocratès had the unfortunate notion of inviting his laboratory assistant to this party: a young woman "as fresh and gracious as she was bigoted and prudish," from the provincial Catholic bourgeoisie, who found herself entirely out of her element at the gathering, as if she had fallen into a trap. They played the bad joke of forcing her to put on a disguise, and to that end concocted the scene that supposedly took place among the insurgents in Barcelona, with Malagrida arranging the tableau vivant down to the smallest details.

"Fine, but why put her in the fresco?" Jérôme asks him.

"To get my revenge," replies the Spaniard.

"To get your revenge? After you insulted her so appallingly?" asks Jérôme.

"Yes. First of all because she made the mistake of being here, where I am."

"How could she be here?"

"She's Sister Théophile, of course!" replies Malagrida. Only then does Jérôme remember seeing the future Sister Théophile in Carpocratès's laboratory. Later we shall see that Sister Théophile had recognized Jérôme well enough—as Malagrida's friend. But until this moment, Jérôme never made the connection. Malagrida had to serve as intermediary.

The painter goes on: "And second of all, to avenge myself—or rather to avenge us, Mother Angélique and me—for Théophile's utter duplicity! She warned the Mother against me when I first asked Angélique to take me in, and she undoubtedly denigrated me to Sister Vincent as well . . ."

The seminarian cuts their meeting short. But this is far from a rejection on his part, far from a dismissal of the *prava cogitata* that assail him. Rather than covering his ears and forgetting the words of this adventurer, who had long since lost all sense of reality for him, Jérôme sees a new terrain open up before his eyes and hurries to speak with Mother Angélique about the measures she must take to protect Sister Vincent from the Spaniard. Could it be that at some unknown time Sister Vincent gave Malagrida reason to hope, perhaps before she took her vows?

* * *

When La Montagne learns that Mother Angélique is hiding Malagrida in her house, he flies into a rage; fearing that Angélique might have reason to secretly nurture Malagrida's passion for his niece, he feels doubly wounded in his own esteem for Malagrida, who so cruelly betrayed him after their pilgrimage to La Salette. La Montagne is in this the victim of a tragic misunderstanding: since each soul has its own *charismas* (those gifts—as he feels more than reasons—received from the Holy Spirit), the responsibility placed upon each soul is that it seek to awaken in another the sources of grace it unknowingly contains. La Montagne numbers among his own gifts that of clairvoyance: he can see into—or believes he can see into—the souls of others. Since his own inner demons ensure that he tends to view his flock in ways that are forbidden, La Montagne has developed a profound sympathy for people in similarly desperate straits, and since there's never a shortage of such crises in his vicinity, this sympathy of his has further encouraged his will to charity, has evolved into a supposedly supernatural sympathy with the souls of men. But even in this psychic sympathy of his, the forbidden desires persist, and these tend to be the deciding factor in choosing the objects of his apostolic fervor. With very young men, La Montagne, despite his inclinations, is able to do good without causing harm: his desires, restrained by devotional discipline, become a pedagogical stimulant. But when his sympathy extends to adults, the resistance with which even the weakest personality will not fail to meet any new influence reestablishes the original conflict: what is forbidden to La Montagne reappears with a new, cherished face . . . And the need to win the beloved over, spiritually speaking, either merges with one's natural penchant to yield to someone behaving with "excessive virility," or else becomes frustrated by the desire to overcome someone acting too passively, trying to shy away.

Plainly the author of *The Suspended Vocation* gave La Montagne a rather tortuous sort of psychology. Caught up in a hodgepodge of psychoanalysis camouflaged as demonology, he has considerable difficulty dramatizing what makes him tick:

"La Montagne, in his relations with Malagrida or Jérôme, did not merely have to overcome the evil forces that he saw churning in them. To dominate them in favor of their *charismas*, he had also to struggle with himself, so that his own demonic powers—after serving their sympathetic purpose—wouldn't wreck the spiritual work that this sympathy had started in their souls. Unfortunately, this is the very moment for which the demon lies in wait in order to insinuate itself; having been involved at the beginning, it also wants to have the last word. La Montagne undoubtedly did want to liberate the spiritual gifts of Malagrida and Jérôme; but this desire was always coupled with an illicit curiosity that focused on the darker portions of their souls. This curiosity, which La Montagne no longer recognized for what it was, because it was the engine of his zeal, found a suitable public face under the name of *fraternal correction*."

Perhaps by setting the disciples of La Montagne and Mother Angélique in opposition, the author intended to show two conflicting doctrines of the soul within the Church in battle. Jérôme can see that La Montagne is drawn to the *charismas* buried in each soul, but his impression is that La Montagne nonetheless provokes in others the forces that counter those *charismas*; it's this, Jérôme tells himself, that makes La Montagne so unable to countenance the simple need dictated by human nature to freely enjoy the exercise of its will before its soul can be informed by grace.

Rather than adopt Mother Angélique's wise counsel, when La Montagne can't reach his precious *charismas*, he prefers the company of darkness, because the obvious merit of these malign forces—demons again—is to offer a *spectacle* such that our pain succeeds in *distracting* us from the profound *ennui* of healthiness. La Montagne thus has his reasons for not pulling the splinter from his paw—or anyone else's: if there are demons present, why bother with *charismas* . . . In the past Jérôme too was much affected by this perspective, but since the seminarian's uncertain association with the Black Party, he has at last learned to distinguish between the natural and supernatural orders of creation. Created nature is a result of grace and is thus excellent in itself; to be sure, there are *traces* of the demonic in it, but these do not prevent grace from becoming a *quality* of the soul. In the end, it's better to wait for this quality to emerge on its own than to attract the attention of the demonic by actively trying to dislodge it: nature, like all things, cannot help but aspire to goodness; one has to avoid handling it too roughly, one has to learn to dress its wounds. This doctrine could have brought peace to Jérôme, but the author will show us that, even here, Jérôme is unable to prevent himself from drawing dangerous conclusions, indeed doing so under an influence that knows how to use even serenity for its own purposes. One of the ideas that has always haunted Jérôme is the notion that a priest ought to be a physician of both soul and body, and it is this delusion, coupled with the abovementioned approach in discriminating between the natural and supernatural orders of existence—which leaves so little room for the demonic in life; which almost seems to dismiss the spiritual nature of evil—that allows the misled believer to see the forces of darkness as entirely unspectacular, in any case separating them from that nonexistent dramaturge known as the devil in order that the physician might restore their proper provenance to the Mind. Is that what the priest Persienne accomplished? Jérôme knows he's a practitioner; has he accomplished this miracle of amalgamating

Doctor Angélique and Doctor Freud? How can he reconcile the administration of the sacraments with the exploration of those vile subjects psychiatrists have claimed for their own? And where do exorcists fit into all this? Must they too remove themselves from the stage, along with all the Evil One's theatrics? Jérôme asks himself these questions when he goes to visit Persienne, motivated less by curiosity than by something we might identify as little more than a lust for power. Any need he might feel to give the Body of the Savior to others is far less present in what he believes to be his perseverance than the certitude he will emerge from his perplexities the day he can himself consecrate bread and wine. The power of consecration is a power over oneself and others; even if Jérôme truly did have the spirit of renunciation and absolute sacrifice in him, a will toward obedience, still there would be this hunger for power in him as well. And what he believes he now sees in the person of Persienne is a priest who adds to the ecclesiastical power of binding and loosing confessions of sin the power not only to bind but also set loose the forces of darkness within us, actually *provoking* the desired confession . . . But this is only one way in which the author interprets the actions of his character: Jérôme is acting in good faith when he thinks that a man commits a crime only when he believes he is doing so.

The priest called Persienne is described to us as "a fellow around sixty, his expression growing almost lewd whenever he was about to seize on some unanticipated understanding of reality, after which he might then burst out laughing at the thought of the sinful men of this world 'going about their merry way,' as though nothing were amiss, after which he might just as well become serious and hold up an index finger while raising his eyebrows above his glasses, not so much demanding that his earlier laughter be forgotten as allowing it to remain in the background, the better to contrast with this apparently severe attitude."

"First of all," says Persienne to Jérôme, "yes, first you must tell me what you *did* in order to have to move from 'one zone to the other,' and what *they* told you when you did?"

"That's exactly what I was going to ask you," says Jérôme.

With each word they exchange, Jérôme sees the image he had created of the Priest-Therapist being erased: no, whatever Persienne is, it isn't that. Little by little, everything becomes banal: in Persienne, the Therapist has consumed the Priest; but having eaten him up, the Therapist, in a very priestly manner, doesn't hesitate in applying his scientific discipline to the Master Himself, not only His disciples—as if the power to separate the Body and Blood has become, monstrously enough, the power to separate the Mind and the Soul. And having broken down the dogmas of the Church as though they were just so many neuroses, Persienne deposits their severed limbs at the feet of the only god to whom he truly bows, a two-faced divinity: sometimes death, sometimes desire; sometimes impulse, sometimes inertia. Strangely, to Persienne's mind, the grand architect of his religion appears to be the same as ever: "We emerge from sleep, we fight against sleep, we attempt to reduce its dominion, yet we must still divide our condition between wakefulness and sleep, a sleep that makes our waking stronger, much as sleep too is made more potent by its alternation with waking, and even as dreams seem to assure us that the two phenomena are one and the same. We wake in sleep, we sleep in wakefulness; then sleep takes over once again, and willingly or by coercion we finally give in. Faced with this inescapable condition, the Master has indicated to us the only possible attitude: that of the Cross."

Jérôme has known for a long time now that a priest could transgress his ministry with every word; what is news to him is that a priest, in the name of the Word that made him a priest, could give himself the authority to *destroy* it. Should he ask Persienne, Why even bother saying mass? and how can you say it? how can you pronounce the consecratory words? But Jérôme keeps these questions to himself. He prefers to ask: What about the people who still believe in the Church? What do you say to them?

"I fortify their faith," says Persienne. "And if they have weakened in their faith, always assuming that it is this weakness that allows them to flourish (to battle sleep, to remain in salutary insomnia), I leave all as I find it. But where it seems to me these souls are unbalanced as a result of their faith itself, I stuff them with all the arcana their faith is able to swallow."

"You mean to say," asks Jérôme, "that you aim to make them leave the Church? To destroy the Church and its dogmas?"

"Nothing could be farther from my mind!" cries Persienne. "The Church alone can teach us the truth as it is and not as how we like to dress it up. Only the Church can teach us about Christ as he was, and not as we think him to be. In a word, it's only the Church that can teach us what I've just told you—because only the Church can make men accept death."

"Plenty of nonbelievers have no trouble accepting it," replies Jérôme.

"No," says Persienne, "they live, that's all. They allow themselves to go on living because they cannot do otherwise. The Church alone, on the contrary, can and must teach them that there is nothing—nothing at all—to hope for from the hereafter, and yet to live nonetheless experiencing all the richness of their souls."

Jérôme isn't too terribly surprised by such a conclusion coming from this mouth: it almost seems to him that he's already heard someone speak these same words. Perhaps that someone is speaking yet again. His curiosity is directed elsewhere: "Do you think," he asks, "that among the high clergy there are those who, thinking as you do, and with this unacknowledged goal in mind, maintain the faith in people's souls by way of a clergy that you would consider more credulous?"

Persienne begins to smile and again breaks into genial laughter. "My child, if it's remained a secret till now then you can rest assured it isn't consciously in the hearts of men. Today everybody believes what they say, and what they say, they believe. The secret, so to call it, lies in the institution itself, it is the very phenomenon of the Church that confounds men and leads them where they must be led. And, for this simple reason, *nothing shall prevail against it.*"

The fact that Persienne would use a divine quotation to deny the divine nature of the institution to which they both belong, and thereby the divinity itself, manages to stupefy our seminarian. How could it be that Persienne's superiors are so totally ignorant of his manner of thinking?

"But," says Jérôme, "what does the Diocese think of your therapeutic activities?"

"What matters," explains Persienne, "is that everything proceed according to the intentions of the Church itself. As for the rest of it, it's simply a matter of keeping out of their way. Do that, and not only will they let you be, they'll even come to you for help."

"In what circumstances?"

"My dear child," says Persienne, "Novice-Masters from various orders, with the authorization of their superiors, sometimes consult me about certain cases in their flocks when they feel they are dealing with situations of . . . equivocality. More often Novice-*Mistresses* than Novice-Masters, I grant you."

"And then?" says Jérôme, half out of nosiness and half out of stupefaction.

"And then," continues Persienne, "I tend to conclude that the symptoms being demonstrated were always going to manifest and indeed ought to have done so much earlier, because in making a decision like giving up the world, retreating to the cloister, or just submitting oneself to the rule of whatever order, in making such decisions think how large a role imagination, obsession, and hallucination must play—in our day and age!—such that in the majority of our ecclesiastical communities, taking say a population of seventy to one hundred people, perhaps ten—I overestimate!—barely *five* could possibly have responded to an authentic vocation."

Jérôme himself feels wounded by this, but he is too strongly intrigued by such reasoning not to agree with it, privately, in the moment, even if he knows he might reject it as false a few moments later. The resentment he nurtures toward those he believes have misunderstood his own vocation inclines him to question the very institution in which he has been unable to find his place.

"How can you ever establish that a vocation is authentic,"

he asks, "when, according to you—if I've understood you correctly—there's no such thing as a voice calling down from above to those believers capable of hearing it, and loudly enough that they feel they must obey? And how can the Church—which, by the way, exists wholly on account of just such a voice, and which has always received those who obey its call—even conceive of consulting a mind like yours, which considers this call illusory, which thinks this voice has never called to anyone at all?"

"I'm not challenging the reality of the phenomenon, nor indeed the edifices in the world that man has built upon it—that's not the issue. I simply attribute this phenomenon to another origin, which I prefer to locate in the powers that inhabit the infinite and irreducible space that is the human psyche. This is why I can get along with the Church to a certain degree, and why the Church trusts me and values my judgment as to whether, in a given person, there might be anything preventing him or her from giving up the world, becoming dead to it, and from adhering wholly to this death without it or the dark garb representing it to other men—not to mention those who have also donned the habit!—becoming a sort of masquerade, a travesty of the true communion that can exist between one part of the soul and another. In a word, in order for there to be authentic vocation—I can't use any other term than the traditional one—in order for there to be a valid answer to this call, we must understand what is really meant when the Master invites us to follow Him. What does *obediens usque ad mortem crucis* mean other than that, with all the obedience of a loving son, He went to the Cross—His nuptial bed—to embrace his Mother, Death . . . an embrace he has invited us to share."

"Do you mean that the Church . . ." asks Jérôme, "Do you mean that Our Holy Mother the Church is only the image of . . ."

"The Church does not say what she is," says Persienne. "But she knows that I know."

When Jérôme, stunned to hear that an atheist priest should be allowed to counsel the true ministers of Jesus Christ, assumes he should report this conversation to his Spiritual Director, the latter begins by doubting Persienne's atheism; from there the Bishop concludes that the consultations of which the Therapist had spoken are all perfectly aboveboard. After all, the Church asks nothing more of the "euthanasic" priest than that he administer to the needy in its Name: whatever his manner of interpreting the sacraments, it's hardly for him to remove the sacerdotal seal with which the actions of a priest, even if he's an atheist, remain imprinted; on the contrary, as soon as man ventures to speak in the name of his own reason (but what is the reason of a man? his soul no more belongs to him than the mark that he bears, and he can have no real knowledge of it, whatever he may say, for all his lucidity)—as soon as he speaks in his own name, he becomes the touchstone of the faith of those patients that the Church deems it useful to entrust to him—a practice far more just than the old procedure of turning them over to the secular authorities. The particular manner in which the "euthanasic" priest conceives of human nature is orthodox to a certain degree; it allows for the usual distinction between the two orders of being, natural and supernatural. Persienne speaks of a human nature untouched by grace. In such a case, teaching man to die is the only thing that can matter to the Church. It is the duty of the Church to teach that man is destined to live only by the grace of the death on the Cross. What is valuable to us, says Jérôme's Spiritual Director, is not Persienne's seeing the grace in a given man or woman— he is quite incapable of that—but rather that his "patients" are informed by grace regardless. Be assured that such souls are impervious to any methods he might apply to them; they are beyond his simple diagnostics. Either grace has truly uprooted pride and planted humility in the soul of one of his patients, or else this soul is simply delighting in precisely the sort of delusion that Persienne will recognize the better for having perhaps allowed himself to fall victim to it.

Jérôme feels caught in his own trap. Suspicious of his own desire for "magical" abilities, he had been hoping his interview with the utterly materialist Persienne might bring him some clarity, but he realizes now that he wanted too to come away with something no less effective to quench his thirst for power—a better understanding of the means by which he might influence himself and others. Jérôme had thought, in short, that he might sign a deal with Beelzebub to drive out demons in the name of God. Instead, Persienne's words prove to Jérôme that he has to choose between them once and for all. The Church itself has already chosen, and because of this it can consider the "atheist" priest as separate from the therapist within the person of Persienne, whereas Jérôme had wanted to merge the two under the instructions of his own sovereign demon. Disappointed, he hurries back to his Spiritual Director to give full vent to his indignation, since this is at least a way to protect himself, or so he thinks, from the demon that plagues him—which he even thinks he sees for an instant, there before him, in the flesh—but expressing this indignation serves only as yet another self-denunciation.

How at ease Jérôme feels in his pride when at the end of their talk Persienne takes him in arms and looks at him as if he has found at long last his only sympathetic disciple, saying, "Be wise and be patient, for two or three more years, and you will in turn act for the highest good of all. Stay firm in your discipline—that is all *they* ask of you." But the author clearly wants to show us Jérôme at his lowest and most lamentable: our seminarian no longer has the strength to follow any guideline whatever, not that of the "euthanasic" priest any more than that of his Bishop. Still, it is undoubtedly Providence that keeps him mired in uncertainty and insecurity: otherwise he might become "much worse than Persienne." Now, how much less at ease he feels when face-to-face with his Spiritual Director—with whom he is nonetheless supposedly united by the same beliefs—when the Bishop places his hands on the seminarian's shoulders and says, "*Are you able to drink of the cup that I shall drink of?*"

Well might we ask why the author supposes it to be so difficult for Jérôme to get himself defrocked. Wouldn't a simple word from the Director suffice to banish him? Why so many detours and precautions? Firstly, we assume, because a forced defrocking always gives rise to ugly and slanderous rumors, best avoided; secondly, however—and this is the real point of interest here—because it is a delicate surgical operation; a defrocking must not lead to revolt, and this is precisely the risk in Jérôme's case. He is asked, instead, to stop playing the role he imagined for himself—no more and no less. He must be convinced that he was, all along, acting a part. This is not, notes the author, a mere question of having or not having an aptitude for a particular job—though think how hard it must already be to make a man who has devoted himself to a career admit that he doesn't have the talent for it!—because no matter the blow to his self-esteem, in these situations, the failure remains exterior to the man himself: it doesn't affect *who* he is and could still become. In Jérôme's case, however, it is indeed the entire man at stake, a man who from one day to the next has felt one of the most intimate regions of his soul stripped bare, leaving it all the more exposed because he not only concealed this aspect of himself, but felt no compunction about doing so; the man who claimed: *where you live, I am dead*, and where you are dead, I live, now has to admit he was *only playing dead* and living much more where he blamed others for living. Jérôme, continues the author, hadn't realized that he'd chosen the most dangerous, most revealing discipline in the world; for the priesthood is no practical profession in which only a part of ourselves need operate, hammering away at some utilitarian task; nor is it like art, in which the drive to express what we are makes it necessary to hide our intentions; no, it is precisely the domain where there is no hiding place save death, because it is the domain of Last Things.

When there is no alternative but a defrocking, when an initiate's departure doesn't result from his own decision, made without coercion, on the basis of his own observations, after recognizing that he doesn't belong wholly to the Church—when such a person doesn't feel closer to the Lord in becoming a simple layperson again, when on the contrary he believes he is losing his special connection to God in so doing, along with the holy responsibilities that he embraced but could not fulfill—then his superiors are faced with a daunting task indeed; and because it requires such infinite patience, even the preliminary steps in this process tend to be avoided. This is why so many novices, lacking sufficient maturity to judge themselves, and moreover surrounded by peers ignorant of any way to help, find themselves one day prisoners of their cassocks, carrying the sacerdotal seal as a slave might bear the brand of a foreign lord. This is just what Jérôme's Spiritual Director wants to avoid happening. The author goes on to give him the following interior monologue:

"This is God's business. We all may have been called—but not all have received the same gifts. In Jérôme, the gift of intelligence, contaminated by an ineradicable pride, has been warped into a simulation of piety. In this state, it's in danger of becoming something more akin to a decrepit debauchee's gluttony for sheer sensation—as we see in that old visionary La Montagne, wanting to roll God's mysteries around in his mouth merely to *savor* their flavor!—whereas an uncorrupted intelligence knows how to content itself with contemplating and finding joy in them. Granted, even this sort of spiritual gluttony and its lust for new and exciting flavors are a degraded form of the appetite for God—but we must find a way to satisfy this desire according to nature, not in violation of it. For his appetites to be purified, Jérôme must consent to humble himself by returning to the natural, original conditions of his existence.

"Yes," the Director says to himself, "he must relearn how to undertake simple, human acts before rising to sacramental ones—those meager human behaviors that so terrify him, because he finds them humiliating. He must learn to work on his own behalf as well as for others, but he will never reach this point until it is made necessary by love; instead of worrying about people's souls, he must first learn to *love* one, and not in the abstract, but face-to-face ... and he must be free to act on this love accordingly! Yes, he must take it upon himself to become an ordinary man—someone like Jérôme can never be too banal. Certainly he will still be playing a role, but in such a case we will willingly pardon him his dissimulation: to force oneself to be average, to live incognito, is also a sort of asceticism."

But Jérôme's Spiritual Director can't claim to know the ways of Providence, and must admit that if Jérôme has become a cleric, God surely wanted it thus—for whatever inscrutable reason. Then again, he also knows that Providence acts only under the cover of our own human wills; if this is so, he must also believe that whatever *plot* he now cooks up to aid Jérôme is also in the great plan. Is he or is he not Jérôme's Spiritual Director? He has to intervene; if he succeeds, well, God will have wanted it so—and if not, likewise. One wonders whether the author intended to stir up some controversy here over the notion of Providence, perhaps even wanting to caricature this idea whereby everything has either been prepared in advance, and events all occur as planned by God, or else each minor player contributes his or her own initiative, unbeknownst to the others. If God has inspired Jérôme's Spiritual Director, he will also have allowed for the reactions of the seminarian, and the author is at pains to show us that while the priest has no illusions about his own freedom, seeing himself as only an instrument, Jérôme believes himself free to act, and in so doing only tightens the knots of his confessor's net. In this we see again the writerly bias of our novelist, determined to sustain the supernatural ambiance in his work by debunking whatever might seem supernatural; but after having most recently attempted an "analytical" exegesis of such forces, now, perhaps carried away by the momentum of his plot, he leaves us wondering whether he's about to give way to the old "Masonic" process of demystification by way of a paradoxical piling on of even more arcana. Is Jérôme's entourage about to try to liberate him from the delusion of his vocation in the same way that Don Quixote's entourage endeavors to open his eyes to reality and heal him, in Cervantes's masterpiece, by outdoing him in madness? One is also reminded of Schiller's *The Ghost-Seer*, in which the Jesuits' "plotting" leads the Protestant prince to convert after first making him fall from superstition into skepticism. Perhaps the author had some memory of these two great models. What might he have accomplished if he'd also had just a little of their genius?

The author considers it useful to show us Jérôme making one last faux-pas: the seminarian, somewhat overwhelmed by all his recent experiences, would like a change of scene. He might thus escape the insinuations aimed at undermining him. Sadly, the author has spoken to us so little of Jérôme's own religious feelings—he almost never mentions him in prayer, never speaks of how Jérôme adapted to his vows—that he now struggles to hold our interest when he suddenly deems it necessary to show Jérôme struck by nostalgia for his earliest days as a novice, regretting the loss of the serenity he used to feel when faced with the Holy Sacrament, that he used to feel locking himself away in his cell: the joy of starting a new and pure life. The author may try to tell us, now, that the only moments of perfect quietude Jérôme ever experiences are during the morning low mass; that he puts almost childish care into preparing the chalice—that source of power!—and that once mass has been said, when he's alone again with the priest, he does everything he can to prolong this state of peace with which he begins his day—but we as readers are rather ill prepared for this. Yes, we're told that it's as though Jérôme stands atop a mountain in the morning and fears his coming descent into the valley of wicked thoughts—but how weak this image is. With everything still in suspense—since nothing's happened yet!—Jérôme can enjoy a sense of oneness in the morning with the purity of the sacred acts he's just completed; he remains concealed—a far more interesting avenue of exploration, had it been developed further—in the performance of those rites by which the Presence Itself is announced. How Jérôme longs to be able, somehow, to extend to all the hours of his life that pass outside the sanctuary, to all the relationships he will have with others there, the atmosphere of those rites in which he belongs fully to his Lord and knows himself to be known by Him; but once he consumes the Host, once he leaves that holy place, he finds himself feeling vulnerable, lacking self-possession, and all the light that penetrated him becomes little more than another object of thought, of curiosity and contestation, a justification for his taking a smug tone with regard to any of his peers who doubt he has ever known this grace (a gift that is perfectly beyond our control, of course, making the author's insistent affirmation as far as Jérôme is concerned sound more than gratuitous here).

What we take away from this is that, since no one is as yet willing to obligate Jérôme to abandon his path, he should at least keep to himself for the time being, even if neither Persienne nor his confessor has yet instructed him to do so—he should avoid Mother Angélique as well as La Montagne, and certainly any chance meetings with Malagrida. What he needs most desperately is to be *seen* in the same manner as he most desperately desires to *see*, and none of these characters are capable of it. Yet he remains unaware that there is indeed someone who takes him seriously, and that she is very nearby. Sister Théophile vainly seeks an occasion to enter into contact with Jérôme: Mother Angélique has often spoken to her of Jérôme's perplexities, though mainly to observe the good Sister's reactions. Théophile, however—presented to us as possessing a good heart and a clear mind—doesn't criticize but rather effuses sincerely over Jérôme's vocation, remembering him as the young man she used to see frequenting a libertine milieu. Sister Théophile soon realizes that the Mother is out to destroy Jérôme's faith in his own vocation. She has no means of intervening aside from ardent prayer, and so makes the seminarian's vocation her daily concern. This undoubtedly robs her of much peace of mind, but Théophile is inspired to raise her pious ambitions on Jérôme's behalf because she will then have an even better reason for defending herself against the unrelenting attentions of the Mother Superior—for whom the aversion she feels will push the young nun to redouble the penances, sacrifices, and mortifications she devotes to the future priesthood of the seminarian. To "correct" her, Mother Angélique, whom this sort of zeal can only displease, rightly or wrongly, soon inflicts counter-penances on her charge, requiring Théophile to dress as a civilian and, under the pretext of undercover work in a zone controlled by the Black Party, exposes her to some rather alarming promiscuities; Sister Théophile's assignment is to lure out suspects—to which of the two camps they are suspected of belonging is no longer clear—to travel with them, find temporary lodgings for them, and bring them food, but she accomplishes her task with no less fervor than her holy obeisance, because, in the end, nothing could be more satisfying to her taste for mortification, her wholly obedient mind, than to submit to the will of a superior she must do her utmost not to despise.

One day, as Jérôme is leaving the Catholic Institute, he passes Théophile in her street garb without being noticed; he walks by her, stops, and turns around, the shock of recognition all the more keen for the fact that he's never seen her wearing anything but the habit of her order. He decides to follow her, at first only intending—or so he tells himself—to figure out the purpose of this outing, when, on a boulevard, he sees her disappear into an alley. He waits for her to reemerge, and the author enjoys describing the seminarian's nervousness, how ashamed he is of himself, the manner in which Jérôme tries to slip away when, after a rather long time, Théophile rematerializes carrying a little painting in a paper bag. A few moments later, in the convent's entryway, Jérôme has ample opportunity to lift a corner of the painting out of its sack and recognize Malagrida's handiwork: a perfectly executed portrait of La Montagne crowned with the papal tiara. The "suspects" about whom Mother Angélique was so concerned apparently came down to a single person: that same damnable Malagrida, whom the Mother has since installed in some garret studio or other. In addition, as Jérôme will later deduce, the Mother, seeking to toughen Sister Théo up, had no qualms whatever about putting the girl into contact with the very individual who'd debased her previously; and Sister Théo, as docile as a somnambulist, taking charity to the extreme, not only took meals to the libertine painter, but was also in charge of passing messages to him and bringing Angélique the answers, evidently without knowing anything about their stratagems. The Mother's evasive response to Jérôme's question about Malagrida's sudden disappearance from the convent proves to him that she still doesn't think it opportune to tell him everything and enjoys excluding him from her secrets almost as much as she enjoys forcing him not to reveal the ones to which he's already privy. Deeply insulted, Jérôme decides to watch for Sister Théo's next outing. This time, seeing her depart, he hurries ahead to guard the alleyway, and steps out in front of the Sister when she attempts to step inside, carrying a basket of provisions. Acting decisively, which is quite out of character, Jérôme approaches Théo and, pretending he has an urgent visit scheduled with Malagrida, offers to take up the supplies, insinuating that he wants to "save her from having to go in there." The Sister does not protest, undoubtedly in order not to offend Jérôme, but she says she must go up anyway, because she has received strict orders, and then because she and Malagrida have become "good comrades": she took care of him during a recent high fever, and she often does his cleaning, since the convent arranged this studio for him, etc. At this point, the author finally gives us a few indications as to Sister Théo's appearance: tall and thin in her well-fitted black coat, with a pale complexion and light eyes, her expression switching from extreme severity one moment to the most perfect impishness the next. Jérôme is about to suffocate from anger and emotion. Malagrida, however, shows no surprise at seeing them arrive together, and as the seminarian looks on astounded, the Sister gives the painter a letter that he puts in his pocket, noting that he will not be dining at home tonight. Whereupon the Sister takes her leave, assuming that the Mother would happily trust Jérôme to receive any messages Malagrida might want to send along. Malagrida now opens his letter and shows no hesitation in commenting on it aloud; it's from Sister Vincent. He tells the seminarian he's surprised that Angélique doesn't confide such messages to Jérôme rather than the nun. He then complains that he doesn't have much more freedom here than at the convent, and that Sister Théo—under the pretext of taking care of his domestic life—has also undoubtedly been tasked with watching him.

"Every day I hope to open the door to 'Vincent,' and it's that rail of a girl Théo I see instead!"

Malagrida's words contain a hidden thorn that pricks Jérôme, because the latter is not unaware that the painter harbors, at best, mixed feelings about Carpocratès's former assistant. Jérôme is disgusted and doesn't know what makes him more indignant: the innocent intervention of Sister Théo or the fact that Angélique is using it to debauch La Montagne's niece.

"She's not made for this life, *amigo mío*," declares Malagrida, who has never hidden anything from the seminarian. But Jérôme rushes out to the street not knowing which way to turn; will he be reasonable and go straight to his Spiritual Director? No, he finds himself unconsciously heading toward La Montagne's villa. He is greeted by the "vociferous screams of a convulsionary" (says the author): "You! You're the one the Mother says is acting as intermediary between this impostor and my niece! You, a future priest! My poor friend, what are you waiting for? Drop that cassock in the trash and go back to secular life!"

It had honestly never occurred to Jérôme, notes the author, that the telephone could play an important role in the conflict between the Devotion and the Black Party, and particularly in both Mother Angélique's and La Montagne's lives. Jérôme tries to explain to La Montagne the sordid trail that led him to Malagrida, but to no avail; he himself no longer believes in his own innocence. La Montagne, who apparently relies heavily on methods of intimidation, now calls Jérôme too an impostor, then bursts into sobs and wants to embrace him. Deeply wounded by La Montagne's first burst of invective, however, and frightened by the nightmare of the physiognomic transitions he's just witnessed in the older man—even if he, Jérôme, was the cause of them— our seminarian flees and finally throws himself at his Spiritual

Director's feet. Once again, he is beaten to the punch by a telephone call: Mother Angélique has just phoned to ask the Bishop whether or not she should now consider his directee—whom she had the goodness to take in—a spy of either the Black Party or the Devotion. Since when does a seminarian make it his affair to keep watch over the comings and goings of her girls? Let the Reverend Father deal with the consequences. The Father nonetheless remains in imperturbably good spirits, and Jérôme thinks he even sees a gleam of satisfaction in his eye. Still, the priest doesn't hesitate to remonstrate with Jérôme for his clumsiness; he should have avoided going up to see Malagrida at any cost. Fearing La Montagne, the Mother now wants to blame the whole affair on Jérôme, whose past dealings with Malagrida are known.

What follows is the demonstration of a procedure, apparently initiated at the highest levels of the Church, intended to *change the seminarian into another man*—a demonstration that tests the limits of the author's imagination, which ties itself in knots out of a desire to convince itself that these latest intrigues, and perhaps all of Jérôme's adventures to date, could have been arranged in advance for just this purpose (but, then again, it could be that the mind only ever comes to grips with facts by playing the fool for them . . .). Again we see the same sort of paranoid delirium that was betrayed earlier in the novel in the author's fantasias regarding Inquisitorial machinations against the so-called sodomites of the Devotion; now at last these delusions succeed in dismantling the entire apparatus behind the spiritual drama to which we've been witness—only real in the author's obstinate imagination, not to mention that of his hero.

"But why were you following Sister Théophile?" the Father suddenly asks Jérôme. "Doesn't the Mother have the right to have her girls do as she wishes?"

"I couldn't fathom why Théophile was making those solitary outings, nor why these would ever include visits to Malagrida's studio . . ."

"Does it upset you that much?" (Jérôme's confessor is clearly aware that the seminarian was altogether too complicit, in his heart of hearts, with Malagrida's old effronteries toward Sister Théo, and so speaks of the subject a little exaggeratedly, so as not to reveal a guilt that has not yet touched the young man's conscience.) "Don't let this upset you any further. By denouncing you to La Montagne, the Mother Superior was merely propping up one lie with another."

Jérôme's confessor informs him that the intrigue between Malagrida and La Montagne's niece was in fact concocted by the painter and the Mother Superior; that they both schemed to throw Jérôme off the track by having Malagrida pretend to beg the seminarian to arrange a meeting with little "Vincent"; how it was only too clear that young Théo was Malagrida's true target, and that he was attempting to provoke her, in one way or another—indeed, on Mother Angélique's most unscrupulous instructions; how the Mother, disagreeing with the positive assessment of Sister Théo by the Novice-Mistress (who herself, for a time, bore that same name), was attempting to arouse the girl's passions and so cause her great difficulty, for "experimental" reasons; how Angélique had surmised from witnessing Théo's mortifications the girl's pious devotion to the seminarian, and how she was seeking to counteract them by inflicting on her just this sort of counter-penance, sending her to take care of the painter's domestic needs, providing him with all the more latitude to distract her; yet how the Spaniard has never yet overstepped the bounds dictated by prudence because he is too dependent on the Mother, who enjoys playing with him like a cat with a mouse; and finally, through it all, how Théo, unaffected by their solicitations, with all the purity of her heart, could not have done better than to foil their machinations by apparent simple-mindedness.

As the Father lays out Malagrida's scenario, he stokes Jérôme's jealousy to a white heat, atomizing and extracting the "Malagrida" that the seminarian carries in the corners of his heart, which the young man now—literally—vomits up.

But if La Montagne was perhaps never all that worried about

his niece, now that he's been made aware of this subterfuge he's all the more anxious about the one he called an impostor—not the seminarian but the painter—because he rejects what he believes to be the false evidence of the latter's complicity: Malagrida hasn't been himself, claims La Montagne, since falling into that woman's clutches. What he now keeps telling whomever will listen is that Mother Angélique has cast a spell on the Spaniard, and if she is trying to compromise Jérôme, it's because she wants to get rid of an inconvenient witness. She is a sorceress, she has bewitched even herself, and she must be freed from her own spell, but this will be possible only if both the painter and the girls of her community are removed from her influence ... "In the meantime, the better to snare her, we will pretend to take her latest scheme at face value"—and well might the characters claim to only "pretend" this, says the author, since everyone remains on the brink of being seduced by her all over again. Jérôme first and foremost, so tragically influenceable, to whom La Montagne has just made the above proposal, is ready to trust him again if only he can bring Malagrida back to the fold. But Jérôme, despite her slanderous accusation, allows himself to be moved by the apparent remorse of the Mother, who now wants the seminarian to believe that her telephone call to La Montagne was entirely his invention, a lie intended to provoke a fit of jealousy in the seminarian; to regain Jérôme's trust, she declares that his presence in her convent is more indispensable than ever and that she has an important project for him (feeling herself on shaky ground, Angélique wants to cloud the water one last time). Under the strictest anonymity, to escape Inquisitorial censure, they will publish a sort of monograph in pamphlet form explaining the fresco; only the Mother and the seminarian will be involved in drafting it. Jérôme will speak to his own ideas about the proliferation of folk devotions as harmful to the True Faith, while Angélique will argue in favor of marriage for priests. Malagrida will print it himself using a handpress and will illustrate it with emblematic images. Jérôme accepts, not only because the project flatters his ambition, but because the Mother is tacitly offering him an obvious opportunity to get between the painter and Sister Théo. But, having sensed the encroaching threat to her powerful position—or possibly wanting to have done with the religious life herself—the Mother intends to depart, causing as great a conflagration as possible. As Jérôme sets to work, believing he's alone in conspiring with Malagrida and the Mother, the latter is actually making the same proposition to all and sundry, presenting it to each in a different, favorable context, and each time—bound by secrecy—her interlocutor believes himself to be her only collaborator. Soon it seems everyone is in the same boat, believing themselves and Mother Angélique to be acting alone. She need no longer even concern herself with the wrath of La Montagne, since he too has been brought in—accepting her offer for reasons we shall soon explore—unbeknownst to Jérôme. Even members of the Black Party have promised, individually, to take part in the monograph scheme, and so the Party itself has been made aware of what's happening. The Party encourages the project because (and here we see how the Mother has been improving her tactics) they see it as a way of getting La Montagne as well as the Devotion to provide intelligence—whereas, in their turn, the adepts of the Devotion, as well as its primary promotor, believe they now have their hands on a weapon to be used against the Black Party. But Mother Angélique can't foresee that she will get caught in her own net, and doesn't count on the chance or deliberate meeting of several of her initiates—each one saying he has a secret, but none of them daring to break their word. Until someone finally conjectures that their secret is one and the same.

Are we to surmise from this that the author wants us to believe that the Church employs the same methods as an intelligence agency? Or that, perhaps, the latter is only one of numerous secularized replicas of the Holy Inquisition in the wider world? When Jérôme, who still suspects nothing, is summoned by his Spiritual Director to serve at a low mass for the intention of *Mother Angélique* the following morning, he is both disconcerted and alarmed. Firstly because he "seems" to have made a "resolution," of which we shall hear more presently; he bitterly regrets having delivered his text to Malagrida, for, in the light of this "resolution," what use will his supposed anonymity be? And then, secondly, what could this sudden need to hold a mass for Mother Angélique portend? Leaving the convent annex where his room is located, Jérôme passes through the parlor and runs into Sister Vincent. He asks after Mother Angélique. The Sister stares, surprised that he is unaware of the most recent developments. She declares that the entire community has been secularized at the command of the Superiors and, fearing she has revealed too much, advises Jérôme to say nothing about this to anyone. He will see the Mother herself as soon as she returns from her outing with Sister Théo. And since neither one nor the other appears for the rest of the day, Jérôme spends the night awake, only falling asleep at dawn and arriving late at the chapel in his Spiritual Director's monastery. Mass has already started and the officiating priest is reading the Gospels; those present are standing, and in the shadows, Jérôme spots La Montagne on one side, and on the other, along with a few girls from the convent, Sister Théo—and his own Spiritual Director. Jérôme hastily pulls a surplice on over his cassock and goes to the altar as the priest uncovers the chalice and raises it up. Jérôme, seeing him in profile, feels he might as well have been struck by lightning: it's *him*, despite his hair cut into a tonsure; those are his flamboyant black eyes, that's his long emaciated face, even though he's shaved off his little mustache. Jérôme anxiously waits for the *Orate fratres* gesture to look at him face-on, extending his arms, and yes, it's still *him*; and now he's going to speak with *his* mouth the words of the consecration; it is thus *he* who holds that power to which Jérôme has aspired through all his torments! Is it possible that *his* long supple fingers, which Jérôme so recently beheld with distrust, that *his* fingers are touching the Body of Our Lord, which he is now offering to Jérôme? That *he* is placing the Presence of the Word on Jérôme's tongue? Jérôme, sweating with emotion, feels like screaming for air, overtaken by such dizziness during the actions required for the final moments of the service that he needs the last drop of his strength to remain standing. The mass is said, the last Gospel read, and Jérôme dares to look at *him* again: kneeling close by as *he* recites with eyes closed the final prayers. Soon *he* rises, pulling his white hood over his head, waiting for Jérôme to precede him into the sacristy. Jérôme feels the need for support and looks for Sister Théophile in the pews, but no longer sees her among those present, and he shudders as *he* observes him do this. They enter the sacristy, closely followed by Jérôme's Spiritual Director, and as Jérôme hears the Bishop behind him pronounce the name, "Inquisitor of the Faith Dom Malagrida," the suave voice of the Spaniard, very close to his face, murmurs the words:

"*We struggle not against flesh and blood, but against the spiritual power of wickedness in high places.*"

How is it that the author didn't realize that this dramatic coup might wreck the already straining machinery of his little drama? wonders the reader, so used to this gag from detective novels. How could he possibly expect us to "swallow" the idea that a monk, whatever his talents, and whatever respect his piety might have inspired in high places, would be assigned by the Holy Office a mission as indecent as that of playing the role of a libertine avant-garde painter, for the sole purpose of penetrating licentious environments on the one hand and monitoring vast layers of the society of believers on the other, under the pretext that these opposed milieus have become mutually permeable? We can accept that a monk is a highly talented painter; we can even stretch credulity to the point of believing that he might have had the time to involve himself in various artistic movements, to put on exhibitions, to compromise himself in scandals; but can we imagine Malagrida's behavior, his words—even if dissimulated—coming from a monk? Can we truly believe in a monk making a mockery of objects of faith, pretending to commit sacrilege when there's no need to? Perhaps the author would answer: *And why not? Malagrida is the Inquisitor!* But if this false libertine was the Inquisitor all along, wouldn't Mother

Angélique, far from recognizing herself as a monster of duplicity, claim that she too was honorably carrying out her mission? If our temporal authorities must learn to move among criminals, the better to combat them, might it not be the case that our spiritual authorities are obliged to adapt themselves to the world of heretics and infidels? Yet where is it written that because the Prince of Darkness may pass himself off as an Angel of Light, the Angel of Light must therefore cloak Himself in Darkness? But perhaps the author means to suggest that our incomprehension is precisely the same as Jérôme's and Mother Angélique's, and that if, in the mouth of the Father of Lies, the truth is always a falsehood, a lie is always the truth in the mouth of Truth.

But the author would also likely say that our objections are beside the point, given that his true purpose lies elsewhere. The simple fact of identifying in the person of Malagrida the Inquisitor whom Jérôme both fears and seeks, the priest whom he aspires to become himself and yet cannot become because he's now crossed the Inquisitor, immediately makes nonsense of everything the seminarian thought he knew. The relationship of Malagrida with Sister Théo is no longer what he understood it to be, but something else, something quite momentous: a spiritual link between the Sister and the Inquisition.

Jérôme now feels rise up in him, as though in a single clot, the words with which he believes he can crush all of them, as they have crushed him: "Usurper of Christ, you won't defeat me!" he cries, but then, mumbling more than speaking, he tries to take back his insult with this circumlocution: "I renounce Rome."

Jérôme's Spiritual Director looks petrified. The monk, fingering the chasuble that he hasn't yet removed, says with a smile on his lips, "Rome, the sole object of my *resentment* . . ."

Such appears to be the nature of Jérôme's "resolution," to which the author alluded earlier. Instead of humbly admitting his failure, he has kept his robes just long enough to throw them in the faces of his superiors, saying, "*You* are the ones who have failed!"

Malagrida places his hands on Jérôme's shoulders and says,

with the same irritating gentleness, "*I cannot hold on to you.* Go to God by the path you think to be the true and right path. But realize too that you don't yet know yourself as you ought, and because you must know yourself, you will come back to us." We can assume that the author means to give the Inquisitor's words a certain significance, since he italicizes them, but Jérôme's dogmatic conflicts have long since ceased to be especially captivating for the reader. Whether the seminarian lapses into heresy or something else makes little difference to us. Why? Because none of this can ever result in any sort of concrete sanction, which robs the story of dramatic tension, since we know the Inquisition doesn't set anyone on fire anymore—contenting itself with igniting hearts. These days, it's far more courageous to leave the Communist Party, thinks the reader, and a narrator recounting *that* sort of story would be sure to be taken more seriously. But perhaps it's here that the import of those italicized words comes in: the story to this point has demonstrated Jérôme's obscure nostalgia for the Inquisition cell, whereas the monk's words, indicating the absence of any external means of constraint, imply that sanction, having become purely internal to the subject—who has learned to judge himself based on his thoughts and to have his actions judged based on his thinking—can have infinitely more serious consequences for one's sense of self than the punishments visited upon their own so-called heretics by the followers of whatever contemporary pseudo-orthodoxy. Since the latter are based entirely on brute processes of intimidation and external threats, if there are initiates or even adversaries dealt with by force who judge themselves and admit guilt by the criteria of these counterfeit churches, it means they are overcome with *animal* rather than spiritual fear. The promotors of these pseudo-orthodoxies are well aware that in the Church alone do the subjects of discipline spontaneously judge themselves and admit guilt as much for their otherwise imperceptible thoughts as for their undiscovered actions, because the most secret part of themselves—what is most unassailable by outside forces—is determined by the slightest movement of their thought.

The Church itself can't know what's happening in the souls of its faithful; as its authority is based in the human heart, the intimate judgment that the pious man delivers in secret upon himself is the basis of the power of the confessional; anyone can enter it, and no one is forced to enter it, but the confessional will subsist as long as the internal judgment that each man applies to himself. The system employed by our contemporary pseudo-orthodoxies can at most lead to one thing: annihilation of thought by physical terror, which merely produces robots. This isn't at all what the promotors of that system wanted; they dreamed of creating proper souls, souls able, precisely, to judge themselves internally and admit guilt before their creators—but the flesh was weak. How horrified they must be at themselves for opening the torture chambers that the Inquisition is only too happy to leave to them.

"Why is he letting me go?" Jérôme asks himself, apparently wanting to be put to the "question." "If he possesses the Truth, why doesn't he do me the kindness of branding it on me with red-hot iron? Shouldn't he at least *lock me up*? At least the Black Party was more consistent!" But the Black Party no longer exists; in fact, it never did. "Jérôme did not suspect," says the author, "that he would in time have both his prison and his branding iron."

The novel, which could end there, contains one last lesson.

Jérôme finds the former Mother in "high spirits"; the stratagem of concealment followed by surprise revelations, which we have been told she made such great use of—and which has now been turned upon her, to her great annoyance, by her superiors—seems to have made her all the more subversive. The Church had been biding its time, waiting for the right moment to act against her, and even then only to liberate her girls, or at least turn them over to a more trustworthy woman; maybe the author means to say here that Malagrida would not have broken cover had he not deemed it necessary.

"No, no, and no," Angélique says to Jérôme. "Malagrida saying a mass for my intention, what a laugh! To think that *they* came to *that* . . ." She has just instructed her girls to choose between her and the order to which they belonged. The fascination exerted by this singular woman is apparently so great that the entire community promptly decides to remain with her. The strangest thing is that to maintain the cohesion and rhythm of their existence, they do not in any way deviate from the rule of the order they have now abandoned; they are dependent on it, it is the basis of their equilibrium, and instinctively all of them recognize it as the most basic expression of the mind of the woman they rely upon to decide what's best for them, even to think for them. Thanks to her method of inciting in her girls vague personal desires, then thwarting them with her authority as Mother Superior, the former Mother Angélique has succeeded, says the author, in totally breaking their will.

"Are all of your girls staying with you?"

"All of them."

So, says Jérôme to himself, Théo too remains faithful to her. When he later learns that, unbeknownst to him, the Mother had approached other prospective collaborators with regard to the secret pamphlet on which Malagrida blew the whistle, Jérôme feels a mad desire for revenge: he will take Théo away from Angélique. And the more he thinks about this vengeance, the further removed he finds himself from theology, polemics, the Black Party, the Devotion—in a word, from any sincere concern with finding his path to God. "And *isn't this* exactly *what was expected of him*," notes the author, who has himself been duped by his constraint of reverse mystification. The more Jérôme thinks of Sister Théo (the author never says *"the former Sister"*), the closer he feels to Malagrida, and the more he regrets his outburst following the mass. And when he finally knocks at the door of his Spiritual Director, Jérôme feels "real relief," and the latter welcomes this return as a "heavenly blessing." Indeed, his "plan" for Jérôme had been compromised by Malagrida's unmasking; the point had been to lead Jérôme to *confession*, but the result of Malagrida's mass was to bury the seminarian's desire to unburden himself under the wreckage of revolt. The author claims that even he can't be certain whether it was Jérôme's Spiritual Director or the monk who had the idea of serving the "inquisitorial" mass. The notion could very well have originated with the monk, considering his taste for theatrics—what could be more natural in this great "painter"—with the Director initially opposing it. Regardless, as a result, Jérôme now seeks to replace the *old Malagrida* in his mind, now having seen him wearing priestly garb. Such may have been the Inquisitor's true aim. When Jérôme at last opens up to his confessor, the latter doesn't just approve what the seminarian confides, he offers to act as his intermediary. The priest will test the waters with Théophile; if she acquiesces to Jérôme's proposal, this will prove she too lacks an authentic vocation. Better still, however, if she hesitates, it would become the priest's duty to nurture this hesitation until he could coax her to the point of a flat refusal. And such a hesitation, notes the author, could be made to last a good long while: Jérôme would then have time to pick at the scab of apostasy with which he believes he's marked himself: that is, either it would harden further in response to a possible refusal by the young woman, or else the seminarian would at last begin to feel the ache of his wound, the true nature of which would be revealed by God. Jérôme's Spiritual Director, having weighed all these eventualities, is depicted fairly rubbing his hands over this new "strategy"—and how absurdly contrived this would all seem if the author didn't at least have the prudence to present the scheme as being perceived through the distortion of Jérôme's new tendency to see a conspiracy lurking behind every cluster of facts. "Anonymous" almost goes so far as to tell us that Mother Angélique's secularization was imposed for the sole purpose of better testing Théo's character and thus making her play the role of Jérôme's spiritual provocateur; but the very idea that the Church might toy with the vocation of a young woman for no other reason than to retrieve a poor lost seminarian is already sufficiently preposterous.

Here then is Théophile, once again a free young woman; yet no less chained, however, in her own mind. Although she's been released from the vows she took so recently in the community of her former Mother Superior, these vows, for her, represent a permanent commitment in spirit: an act of will, regardless of the decision of the Church to render it null and void. She alone can judge the rectitude of her resolution, which she has made the foundation of her existence. Perhaps she will find a new convent and begin again. Or perhaps she will stay with the former Mother, who wants to keep her in what is now merely a home for Amazons under rules whose justification are, at best, obscure. Having taken the second route, for the time being, Théophile finds the unfortunate Jérôme asking for her hand in marriage. This proposal strikes the young woman like lightning—she may be a perfectly incorruptible girl, but she is also bursting with all the susceptibilities of health and youth. She suddenly realizes that she loves Jérôme with a passion heightened by his tormented nature. Isn't it possible that she might save him? She receives his proposal with friendly interest: so well-tempered by that sane doctrine distinguishing between the human order and the order of grace that any repugnance she feels at the nest of vipers concealed within the human order is proportionate to the compassion that fills her for whomever is unable to accede to grace. So when Jérôme's Spiritual Director tests the waters, alluding to the defrocked seminarian's vague desire to renounce his religious convictions, she surprises him with her response: "If something in the practice of our faith has scandalized him, the best thing would be for him to find a way to worship the Lord that does not injure his conscience."

But if, at this stage, she thinks that her deep resolution to maintain her vows will be sufficient defense against Jérôme, she doesn't know with whom she's dealing; Jérôme takes this as a temporary retrenchment at best, which he has every hope of overcoming. Théo soon presumes to discuss their opposing situations; Jérôme then has no trouble showing her the inconsistency of her life with the former Mother Angélique. Théo accepts this argument: she decides she will depart the former convent. But—and here something intervenes, showing us what Théo is truly made of—what she doesn't tell Jérôme, surprising no one so much as herself, is that in leaving the convent she finds herself stripped of her formerly iron resolution: she is on the verge of yielding to him. She is careful not to betray her perplexity so that Jérôme can't claim victory too quickly. What Sister Théophile experiences is a state heretofore unknown to her. She savors her anxiety, doesn't know whether she ought to welcome it as a joy. And she will remain this way for weeks, living within this new state of being: the possibility of loving a man. But this love nonetheless bears the mark of the most terrible infidelity. How could someone who's only ever burned to belong to God alone, someone who has led such a happy conventual life—admittedly in a house as strange as Mother Angélique's—how could she come to see this existence erased?—and moreover, in just a few days? This transformation stupefies her, shames her, and aggravates her perhaps as much as the love she feels developing inside her brings along with it an inadmissible joy, this love that she pushes away but that returns incessantly and that incessantly forces her to sit in contemplation of the ruin of her own self-image. From one moment to the next she wants to give Jérôme her consent, to finally tell him all; maybe God would reappear to her in that moment, reconciled, because God has, after all, left her entirely free . . . or perhaps less God than the Church; but the Church is God, is it not? She need only take a single step, and Jérôme would be happy—but she fears her own happiness. Jérôme neither hopes nor despairs as Théo makes him wait: he doesn't believe for an instant that his desire will ever be granted. For him, everything has come down to this: he made it known to a former nun that he loved her, thus that he desired her, and this declaration had its effect: he succeeded in upsetting her. That Théo might one day belong to him seems like a dream and nothing more; Jérôme is sufficiently overcome by having taken this step. In itself, the step was a legitimate one, but, privately, Jérôme has the most peculiar sensation of having done something infinitely reprehensible: Théo, instead of seeming like a free young woman, will forever be *Sister* Théo for him after all. Thus did Jérôme dare to resort, at first, to a subterfuge that, after everything else that's been said in this story, is not without an element of comedy: his initial proposal is that he and Théo have a *mariage blanc*—this apparently pious solution, honoring Théo's supposed resolution, would also serve as Jérôme's revenge on the former Mother Superior. He proposes, in other words, that Théo remain with Mother Angélique, unbeknownst to whom—unbeknownst to anyone—they would be united. But it is Théo who, full of good sense, counters that a *mariage blanc* "is nothing but a myth"—and that they might as well get married for real. Still, this insinuating proposal of Jérôme's is the final touch in the author's portrait of his character (leaving the reader quite concerned that such a man might ever have been ordained!): Jérôme is fascinated by the reprehensible aspect he gives to a situation that is not in itself reprehensible, but which he wants, at any price, to be blasphemous. This is why, awaiting Théo's decision, he doesn't believe he will ever obtain the impossible thing he's asked for, because having initially asked for something simple in itself, he conceived of the thing he actually wanted—to truly win Théophile's heart—as an impossibility. Yet he will have this impossibility: he knows nothing of what's really going on inside the young woman. Then comes the day when, finally, she admits to him that she's been unable to transcend the vows she once took—abolished by the Church, but still alive within her, before God. Jérôme takes his leave; he got what he wanted, after all—he got to be the tempter, got to play the wicked "Malagrida." He still doesn't suspect his true success when, the following day, he receives the "Parthian arrow": a brief letter from Théophile declaring her love for him as well as the impossibility of this love—because God makes it impossible.

"From that moment on," says Father Malagrida, to whom the author attributes the passages we have just paraphrased, "from that moment on the Jérôme that we had known was dead, his demon exorcised, whereas the natural man within Jérôme had finally learned to love and could open himself to grace; he was cured, from that moment on, and only from that moment, because

Théophile—no longer in his eyes the woman of religion, who she had never really been to begin with—had taken on the reality of a woman who loved him: at that very instant Théophile was *dead* to him, but *alive* for the Lord."

It is time to conclude. We won't blame the author too terribly much for saying nothing about La Montagne's reaction to Malagrida's unmasking himself as the Inquisitor. Must we conclude that La Montagne was also an accomplice, and that his jealousy and worry were also feigned? That the "Devotion of Our Lady of the White Marriage" was no less a fabrication than the Black Party? But we assume the author is exaggerating his material under the pretext of inaugurating his new technique. He claims—as is the wont of certain authors—to have met his protagonist again years later, after all the latter's adventures had concluded, when Jérôme was not only cured, but married. Employing his technique in emphasizing the supernatural by way of the banal one last time, the author implies that Jérôme's wife could have been Théophile's double, at least based on the description we've already received of the nun (undoubtedly altered from her putative, nonfictional model, "to protect the innocent"). This young woman, we're further told, was supposedly the widow of a ship's captain, but it was well known in "high places" that her first husband entered the Trappist order, and that only strict secrecy—a nice bit of casuistry—assured the one the peace of the cloister and the other a lawful human joy. Thus, even Jérôme's happy secular life was apparently kept hanging by a thread: what the Church was willing to keep secret.

Admittedly, our author has a singular way of confusing art with slander. How right is this proverb:

The offender never pardons.

A NOTE ABOUT THE AUTHOR

PIERRE KLOSSOWSKI was a novelist, visual artist, translator, philosopher, critic, and actor. He was born in Paris in 1905 to parents of noble Polish origin; his younger brother, the painter Balthus, arrived three years later. Rainer Maria Rilke, his mother's lover, introduced the young Klossowski to André Gide, for whom he worked as a secretary during the period of the composition of *The Counterfeiters*. Klossowski translated Hölderlin in collaboration with the author Pierre Jean Jouve, joined Georges Bataille in both the review and secret society Acéphale, and flirted with entering a monastery during the years of World War II—an experience recounted and satirized in his first novel, *The Suspended Vocation*. In 1947, Klossowski married the Resistance member Marie-Roberte Morin-Sinclaire, who, lightly fictionalized, became the central figure in his trilogy of erotic-philosophical novels known under the collective title *The Laws of Hospitality*.

Klossowski appeared in Robert Bresson's film *Au hasard Balthazar*, collaborated with the Chilean expatriate Raúl Ruiz on two films for television—including an adaptation of *The Suspended Vocation*—and starred as his own character Octave in Pierre Zucca's film *Roberte*, which adapts scenes from the *Laws of Hospitality* novels.

Klossowski died at the age of ninety-six.

A NOTE ABOUT THE TRANSLATORS

ANNA FITZGERALD is a writer and translator born in Billings, Montana, who lives in Avignon, France. She has translated the work of Robert Pinget and Olivier Cadiot, among others. Her poetry has been published in the anthology *Bright Bones* and in *Les Cahiers du Museur*, *Ollave—Préoccupations*, and *la main millénaire*.

JEREMY M. DAVIES is a writer and editor living in New York. He is the author of the novels *Rose Alley* and *Fancy*, and the short-story collection *The Knack of Doing*.